D1302636

Dream House

Dream House

Christina F. York

Five Star • Waterville, Maine

This novel is a work of fiction. Names, characters, places and incidents are either the product of the author's imagination, or, if real, used fictitiously.

First Edition, Second Printing.

Set in 11 pt. Plantin by Elena Picard.

Printed in the United States on permanent paper.

Library of Congress Cataloging-in-Publication Data

York, Christina F.
    Dream house / by Christina F. York.—1st ed.
      p. cm.
    ISBN 1-59414-235-1 (hc : alk. paper)
    1. Dwellings—Conservation and restoration—Fiction.
2. Dwellings—Maintenance and repair—Fiction. 3. Home ownership—Fiction. I. Title.
PS3625.O74D74 2004
813'.6—dc22   2004048403

This book is dedicated to four people whose real-life love stories, still strong after more than fifty years, set an example for all of us.

To Jerry and Jeanne, who taught me
that love isn't always easy,
but is always worthwhile;

and

To Jim and Mott, the world's greatest in-laws,
who helped make my own dream house a reality.

Acknowledgements

Buying a "fixer upper" is a precarious undertaking, and I want to thank the people who have given me a first-hand look at the process: Dean Smith and Kris Rusch, whose continuing projects have shown the way, and my husband, Steve, who is taking our house from "fixer" to "dream." The experience has been priceless.

Finally, my thanks to the late Kent Patterson for his friendship and motivation. I knew you would come back and haunt me if I didn't finish this one.

Chapter 1

"This is listed as a 'fixer-upper,' " Marty said, as she led the Hortons up the front walk, "but all it really needs is a little cosmetic help."

The little rambler was like its neighbors, a tract house built in the boom that followed the Second World War. There were millions of them, nearly identical, in cities across the country. Here in Eugene, they had been starter homes for returning veterans and their young families, or for the faculty members who wanted to be within walking distance of the university.

Now, decades old tree roots cracked the sidewalk along the blocks of once-identical homes. Most of the returning vets had left long ago for other homes. Many of the houses had been added to, remodeled, repainted, or replaced. From the street, it appeared as though this one hadn't been changed. But it hadn't been taken care of lately, either.

Mrs. Horton sniffed, as though the scrubby yellow grass of the front yard gave off a bad odor. Mr. Horton looked skeptical, but they followed along docilely, waiting to be convinced.

Marty stifled a sigh. Although it was early evening, the heat was still in the 80s. The house would be stuffy and overheated, its rooms too small to allow proper ventilation, and the Hortons would pick it to pieces.

She lifted her curly red hair off the back of her neck, wishing for about the fiftieth time that she had had the foresight to wear it up today.

This was the fourth house they'd seen this afternoon, and none had been to their liking. Mr. Horton was nearing retirement, and he didn't want anything that needed repair. Mrs. Horton insisted on a place where their grandchildren could play. Neither one had seen a kitchen they could agree on, and Marty could feel the temper that went with her hair starting to simmer.

She noticed the beat-up white van parked in the driveway, and the open front door. There wasn't supposed to be anyone else showing the house today, but things always changed at the last minute.

Good, she thought with a twinge of wickedness, let the Hortons think they were about to get beat out on this one. Might do them some good.

As they mounted the two small concrete steps to the front door, Marty hoped whoever was in the house had opened some windows. At least then it wouldn't be quite so hot. She swung back the wood-framed screen door and they went in.

"William," Mrs. Horton said, "this is just like the house we bought when you got out of the service. Remember that place?"

"How could I forget it? I spent half my weekends trying to repair the so-called improvements those idiots we bought it from had made." He glanced around, as if looking for similar problems. "I'm not young enough to do that again," he said, glaring at his wife.

Mrs. Horton lapsed into an embarrassed silence, while William glowered.

Marty had watched the Hortons for three weeks. This was different from their usual pattern. Up until now, Mrs. Horton had immediately dismissed every house, and Mr. Horton had at least feigned interest.

Now, Mrs. Horton seemed interested, and Mr. Horton was frowning for the first time. She felt the adrenaline rush that told her this could be The One. She would have to proceed carefully.

She walked them through each of the three bedrooms, pointing out the sound structure of the house, the lath and plaster walls, and the upgraded plumbing in the main bathroom. She had noted all the features in the listing, knowing she would need to counter the generally dowdy look of the place.

"I know it needs some brightening up," she remarked as they examined the tiny bathroom adjoining the master bedroom. "But it wouldn't need major repairs. Just think about what can be accomplished with a coat of paint, or wallpaper, and some new carpet. Replace these heavy drapes with mini-blinds to let in the light. And the dining room," she led them back down the hall, "has a fabulous southern exposure. During the winter, the room will be full of light in the morning." Right now, she noted grimly, it would probably be a hellhole.

She wondered when they would run into the people from the white van.

They continued through the living room and dining room, and into the kitchen. With each turn, Mrs. Horton recalled another wonderful thing about their old house, and Mr. Horton remained silent. Marty took this as a good sign. If Marty could sell Mrs. Horton on the house, she in turn would sell it to Mr. Horton.

Still frowning, but more in concentration than annoyance, Mr. Horton turned on the hot water tap. Nothing happened. The frown turned into a scowl, and he reached for the other tap.

Hurriedly, Marty dug for the listing. The utilities weren't supposed to be shut off. A wave of relief passed over her as Mr. Horton turned the cold tap, and water gushed into the sink.

"It does say something here about the water heater," she said. "They're planning to . . ."

She was interrupted by a stream of unintelligible shouts from the basement, interspersed with occasional strings of profanity. Heavy footsteps pounded up the stairs, and a dark-haired man in a soaking-wet pair of blue overalls barged through the basement door, still cursing.

"What in the hell do you think you're doing?"

His face was flushed, gray eyes flashing with anger, wet hair plastered to his head. He held a pipe wrench clenched in his beefy right hand, where a fresh gash was beginning to ooze blood. He walked across the kitchen, turned off the tap, glared at the three of them, and stomped back down the stairs.

He stopped halfway down to yell back, "And don't turn it on again!"

They stood in shocked silence, listening now to the small noises coming from the basement. They heard the scritch of metal on metal, a grunt of effort, and the creaking protest of bolts turning after too many years of immobility.

"We'll think about it," Mrs. Horton said, heading for the front door. But Marty knew she'd lost the sale.

What was that idiot doing in the basement anyway?

Will reached the bottom of the basement stairs before he realized he was bleeding. He sucked on his knuckle, as water dripped off his pants and into his shoes.

What were those people doing in the house, anyway? George Lane had assured him it wouldn't be shown this week, so he could do the plumbing he had planned.

He examined his knuckle, and shrugged. A little skin. No real damage, except to his dignity. His reaction was understandable; he hadn't expected anyone, and the sudden rush of water had startled him.

But he wasn't a hot-headed teenager anymore and he liked to think he had learned some self-control over the years.

The scene in the kitchen replayed in his head, as he went back to work on the balky pipe. His skin crawled as he realized how he must have looked to the group in the kitchen—a wild-eyed man in soaking overalls, yelling and bleeding. He must have startled—or frightened—all of them.

Fortunately, he would never have to see any of them again.

Chapter 2

"I swear to you, Beth, I didn't even know he was there, much less that he was working on the pipes. The agent knew we were supposed to show the house, and he lets this jerk come in and tear up the plumbing . . ." Marty shook her head and picked up her drink.

The Mexican restaurant where she and Beth met that afternoon was part of a chain, but the margaritas were good, the bar was air-conditioned, and the prices were reasonable. For today, that was enough.

Beth nodded sympathetically. "It's amazing what owners will do to you. They want the house sold this instant, but will they cooperate? Hell no. They refuse to get the lawn reseeded, and you lose the sale before the clients are even out of the car.

"Or they don't do any repairs until you're busy telling someone how solidly-built the place is."

"Remember that Victorian on Pearl? I'm telling this yuppie couple it would make a perfect B&B, when all-of-a-sudden, wham!" Beth slapped her carefully manicured hand against the tile tabletop. "A huge chunk of the living room ceiling fell to the floor. I swear, it didn't miss the wife by more than three inches. Took another six months to find a qualified buyer." She raised her glass in a mocking toast.

"To the home sellers of the world, may they someday get a clue."

Marty laughed. Beth's theatrical storytelling, her expansive gestures, and her ability to top any bad-luck story on a moment's notice, was working its magic.

Already Marty was feeling better. She knew there were a few more houses around town that would appeal to the Hortons. Eventually, she would find them their dream house. And find herself a decent, and much-needed, commission.

She took a tiny sip of the margarita, savoring the coolness in her throat, licking the salt from her lips. Even if she wasn't driving, her dwindling bank account limited her to a single drink tonight.

Marty leaned back against the tall wooden chair. Beth had cheered her up, the way she had ever since they met, ten years earlier, working in the same real estate office. Beth left for a firm specializing in commercial real estate, but their friendship had stayed.

Marty dipped a salty tortilla chip in the chunky salsa. One of the many things she and Beth agreed on—restaurant chips needed more salt, and even the so-called hot sauce wasn't hot enough.

Marty sat with her back to the entrance. She preferred it that way, allowing her to retreat from the crowd around her. Beth, on the other hand, wanted to watch who was coming and going, and always sat facing the doorway.

Marty admired her friend's boldness, wishing she could invite attention the way Beth did. But she didn't have to discourage a lot of yo-yos, either. Reserve had its good points.

"Marty, whatever you do, don't turn around. There is a real knockout in the entry, and he's looking at you." Beth looked away from the door, shooting a knowing glance at Marty. "Don't give me that look. He is. Really."

"It's one of those don't-I-know-you-from-somewhere looks."

Marty rolled her eyes. This wasn't the first time Beth had been sure some man was looking at her. Usually it turned out to be a nearsighted jerk who thought she was "that cute little redhead in accounting."

She had begun to suspect there was another small red-haired woman in Eugene who worked in an accounting department. If so, she felt sorry for her—half the jerks in town seemed determined to hit on her.

"Sure, Beth. What odds do you want that he'll come ask me if I work in the accounting department? You know how this works." With a studied casualness, she leaned forward and took another tortilla chip. Despite Beth's warning, or perhaps because of it, she had to look.

Trying to appear natural, she turned slightly, glancing over her shoulder at the "knockout" Beth was talking about. He wore artfully-wrinkled linen slacks, a polo shirt, and canvas slip-ons with no socks. A casual look that probably cost more than her entire week's wardrobe.

He did look familiar.

Remembering names and faces was one of the things that made her a good saleswoman, but she couldn't place him right away. His dark hair was neatly combed, cut short-but-not-too-short. He had the kind of expensive tan that comes from long hours on a golf course, and the air of someone who knew he belonged at the top.

But there was something about him that didn't fit. If she could just figure it out. Then she did, and nearly dropped the salsa off of the chip and into her lap.

"Beth!" Marty whirled around, before he could see her.

"It's him! From the house. But he looks so different all cleaned up and dressed like that. I mean, I just saw him for a minute, in overalls and soaking wet, but I know it's him."

"Well, if that's a handyman, I may need to get some repairs done around my place." Beth winked at her. "Can I call you for the name of the construction company?"

Beth paused, an appraising look in her eye, as she studied the man over Marty's shoulder. "Whatever it is, business must be good. Believe me, I know what those clothes cost. I paid for enough of Richard's."

Beth's laughter held a brittle edge. It had taken her three years, and two extra jobs, to recover from the financial excesses of her runaway ex-husband. Marty had to admit Beth knew men's clothes. She had paid for Richard's extensive wardrobe, until his last shopping spree. The shopping, and the marriage, exploded in a shouting match that ended with Beth throwing his beloved clothes in a heap on the porch of their duplex, and locking the door.

"Beth, get serious. He acted like an overbearing jerk. I can't imagine why anyone would want him around, and I sure wouldn't want him near any of my clients. Not unless I wanted to kill a deal." Marty settled with her back to the entrance, her shoulders pulled forward slightly, effectively shutting off any approach. "Just let me know when he gets seated, so we can get out of here without him seeing me. It's too damned hot for another confrontation."

"Well, I wouldn't mind confronting something like that, preferably up close and personal. He really is gorgeous. And that smile . . ."

"I didn't see him smile," Marty said. "In fact, about all he did was snarl. It wasn't what you could call attractive."

"He's turning this way, Marty. He's going to come over here."

Marty ducked her head lower, and stared at the tabletop. She wished he would just go away, or ignore her. She didn't want to talk to him, and she was sure he wouldn't want to talk to her, once he realized who she was. She sipped at her margarita, and looked up at Beth.

"Is he coming this way?" Marty asked.

"No. He's just standing in the entry, looking around. But every time he looks this direction, he stops to look at you." Beth sighed dramatically. "I honestly don't know what it is you have Marty, but I wish you'd give me a little of it."

"Beth, stop it, please? Let's talk about something else. Okay?" Marty's voice edged up, pleading.

"Sure, Marty. Sure. Whatever you say." Responding to the edge of panic in her friend's voice, Beth launched into a story about her boss, and soon Marty had forgotten about the man in the lobby, and was laughing again.

"And then—" Beth stopped abruptly. Her eyes widened. She smiled in a too-wide, show-off-my-caps way, and sat up a little straighter.

Marty thought she was going to wave at someone she knew. She turned to see who Beth was looking at, and saw the man she thought of as "the handyman" walking in her direction. He was accompanied by another well-dressed man, and they appeared to be deep in conversation.

Marty braced herself, unsure how she would respond when he spoke to her. Beth was right in calling him a knockout. He was tan and fit, and he had a cute smile. Maybe, if he apologized, she would invite him to join them. She shot a quick, questioning glance at Beth, who gave her a short nod of encouragement.

Marty turned back to the two men. But instead of finding them approaching her table, she watched in surprise as they turned aside and took two stools at the bar on the opposite side of the lounge.

When Marty looked back at Beth, she could feel an embarrassed blush creeping across her cheeks. Soon they were flaming, announcing her humiliation to everyone around her. She felt as though everyone must be looking at her, wondering why she had been ignored.

"Oh, God, am I embarrassed," she said to Beth.

"Why?" Beth tossed her hair back, and leaned forward in her chair. "He didn't speak to you. So what? Wasn't that what you wanted?"

"It was. But then I thought he was going to talk to me, and I acted like he was . . . I don't know. I feel like such a jerk. I'm sure everybody saw him ignore me." She hunched back over her drink, stirring the pale green liquid with the short plastic straws.

Beth laughed, but stopped quickly as she realized her friend was serious. "Marty, I don't know where you get your ideas sometimes. Nobody noticed anything. They're all too busy trying to *get* noticed to pay attention to who anybody else is noticing or not noticing."

"Oh, Beth, it's all so easy to you isn't it? But every time something like this happens I feel like I'm back in junior high, sitting out every dance while the popular girls laughed at me and danced all night." Marty shook her head, still staring at her drink.

Beth reached across and patted Marty's hand. "Charlie gave you a real kick in the ol' self-esteem, didn't he? Brought back all that crap. But it's ancient history, kiddo. You can't let it, or him, run your life."

Marty nodded. She knew Beth was right. With an effort, she forced her lips into a smile. But she still felt foolish.

★ ★ ★ ★ ★

Will walked with George Lane through the crowded reception area, into the equally-crowded bar, ignoring the press of people around him. Although it was a weeknight, the heat had driven what felt like half the population of the city into this faux-tropical, air-conditioned sanctuary.

"I owe them, George," he said, settling on a bar stool. "They rented that house to a wild kid off one of their construction crews, and let me work off the rent during term breaks and over the summer. Without their help, I probably never would have made it through the university."

He left the rest unsaid, knowing George could fill it in for himself. Without the Bakers, the best Will could have hoped for was a shot at a foreman's position. Instead, he was one of the most successful real estate developers in the region.

"If I can get them a little more for it, then I want to keep working on the place until it sells."

George shook his head at Will. "Why don't you just give them something yourself? You can certainly afford it."

Of course he could afford it. But that wasn't the point. "They won't let me, George. I tried. Every Christmas I send a check, every year it goes uncashed. I ask about it, Betty blushes, and John just shrugs."

"Why not hire it done then? Get it done quickly, and be through with it?"

"They refuse to let me do that. I don't feel right getting workmen in there without their permission. They'll go along with a few things—a plumber or electrician, if I can convince them they're absolutely necessary—but that's about it."

"But they can't turn down a better offer for that old rental." Will sighed. "They're the closest thing I have to a family, George. It's the least I can do."

"I suppose," George answered, though his doubt was clear in his voice.

"You'd do the same for your folks, George." There was a hint of challenge in Will's tone, daring George to disagree with him.

"Okay, okay. Have it your way." George turned away and signaled the bartender for a couple beers. "Can you believe this heat?"

Marty turned on the air conditioner, kicked off her sandals, and ran back the messages on her answering machine. Her dentist, reminding her that she had a cleaning scheduled next week. The cable company with a special offer on HBO. Beth, wondering why she was late for dinner, with sounds of canned Mexican music in the background.

Finally, the answering service, letting her know the Hortons had canceled their appointment for tomorrow morning. Not that she blamed them; this afternoon's performance would have put off a lot more dedicated buyer than Mrs. Horton.

By the time she had reached the end of the tape, the air conditioner had begun to pour out frigid, vaguely metallic-tasting air. She fought off the desire to plop in the papasan chair in front of it with a mystery novel and a bowl of Cherry Garcia.

Living alone held myriad temptations, and she had given in to too many of them after her divorce. Beth had been there for her, holding her together after Charlie had walked out. Unlike Richard, Charlie hadn't argued, or shouted. He just stayed out later and later, until one day he didn't come home at all.

Ice cream and fictional murder had become her retreat.

It wasn't until she realized she was mentally renaming each victim Charlie that she had curtailed her compulsive mystery reading and started seeing a therapist.

As she moved around the small house, she kept thinking about the handyman. Beth was right, he was attractive, though he was older than she had initially thought. When he came bellowing up the stairs, she figured him to be her age. But seeing him later, carefully, and expensively, dressed down, she moved her estimate up. He was probably forty to her thirty-two. Though he obviously took good care of himself, there was a touch of gray at the temples, and laugh lines around the mouth that took years to develop.

She loaded the washer and wondered who he was. Dusting the bookcase, she decided that whoever he was he took himself too seriously. Beth would say she was assuming too much, but he hadn't bellowed at Beth.

Moving clothes from the washer to dryer, she made up her mind to talk with the listing agent in the morning. There was no reason for him to be there when the house was shown by appointment, and she was sure the listing agent wouldn't be happy that his boorishness had cost them a sale.

Having made a decision, and completed her housework at the same time, she gave herself a reward. A teacup of Cherry Garcia, and two chapters of *Skin Tight* before bed.

Chapter 3

Marty pushed open the door to the Home Masters real estate office where she worked. She could smell fresh coffee, and an undertone of Lemon Pledge. Last night was Tuesday, the night the cleaning crew made their weekly rounds.

Lorraine was already at her desk, intent on a telephone call, and Marty could see the big airpot already in place at the coffee station. Setting her briefcase precariously atop the piles of papers on her desk, she grabbed her "Million Dollar Club" coffee mug and carried it to the pot.

Bringing back a steaming cup of black coffee, she returned to her desk, put the battered brown leather briefcase on the credenza behind her, and thumbed the latches.

She took a hard look at the nicks in the case, and the worn patches, and wondered how much longer she could get away with carrying it. She had paid far more than she could afford for it—or rather, Charlie had paid far more than they could afford for it.

She could still remember the flash of anger and childish revenge that had pushed her into buying it, after Charlie told her to "pick yourself out a nice gift" to celebrate when she passed the real estate exam. She had put it on his MasterCard, and he had winced when he got the bill. Still, he had paid it and said nothing.

Her therapist later explained to her that she was trying to provoke him, to get a response, any response, out of him. But Charlie had passive-aggressive down to a fine art. He had simply withdrawn a little further, until, finally, one day he just wasn't there.

Now she couldn't decide whether continuing to carry the briefcase was a symbol that she had survived the break-up, or whether it was a constant reminder of her failure.

She shrugged. Either way, it probably wasn't real healthy, and she would have to replace it someday. Sooner, rather than later, her conscience said.

Turning back to her desk with the multiple-listing book in her hands, she located the name of the listing agent for the house on Agate that she had shown the Hortons. She called the office and left a message for George Lane to call her back.

She missed Lane's return call later that afternoon, and he in turn was out when she called back. She hated the game of telephone tag, hated that it ate up so much of her office time, leaving messages for people who would always call back when she was out. She finally asked the receptionist to take a message, and briefly explained the problem with the handyman, and his behavior toward her and the Hortons.

"You know how it is, some clients get put off by the little things." The woman at the other end of the phone murmured an agreement. Marty could hear her pen scratching against the paper as she wrote. "I really think they were ready to make an offer, and the guy in the overalls blew it for me—for us.

"And you might want to mention the front yard. Most of the yards on that block are pretty nice, but that one needs water, at the very least, and it could sure use some kind of flowers or plants to soften the front, since there's such a tiny porch."

She waited until the pen scratching stopped again. "Anyway, I appreciate you taking the time to get this down. Tell Mr. Lane he doesn't need to call me back, I just wanted to let him know what's happening to his listing." She listened for a moment. "Thank you. You've been great. Bye-bye."

Marty hung up, satisfied she had done the right thing. She would find another house for the Hortons, but this house could become a personal challenge. There was so much potential, she wanted to be the one to find a buyer for it.

Someone who could see in it the things she saw.

When Ralph Gordon breezed into the office the next Monday morning, Marty greeted him with a grin and a hug.

"It's good to see you, Ralph. Are you looking for something, or did you just stop by to harass me?"

Ralph's square, freckled face split into a wide grin. "Now you know you love me, girl. Why keep on pretending?" He dropped his heavy frame into the wooden visitor's chair across the desk from hers, and ran his stubby fingers through his short, sandy hair.

Marty could see that he'd been spending a lot of time in the sun—his hair was bleached lighter than usual, and there were more freckles across his cheekbones and his thick forearms.

"You're looking pretty good for an old man. Want a cup of coffee?" Without waiting for a reply, Marty got two mugs from the coffee station and carried them back. Handing Ralph his, she smiled. "Cream and two sugars, right? Now, what can I do for you?"

"See? You remember how I take my coffee. If that isn't love . . ." He let his voice trail off, and took a sip from his mug.

Marty grinned at him and shook her head. "That isn't love, Ralph. That's salesmanship. Now what is it you *really* want?"

"Well, it's like this . . ." Marty knew what was coming. Ralph was bored with the house he bought last year, and wanted to buy a new one. It was a pattern she knew well. He always bought something that needed work, and when the work was done he tired of it quickly. Soon after, he'd find himself a renter, put the property into his growing pool of investments, and start looking for another place to live.

"I want a place to settle down this time. Something I don't have to work too hard on. I'm not getting any younger, which you keep reminding me, and I feel like I need to put down some roots."

She watched him twist the empty mug in his hands. There was something more to his visit, something else behind his request, but he would tell her when he was ready. In the meantime, she would have to take his story at face value.

She pulled a piece of paper toward her, and started making notes. "How many bedrooms this time? Baths? Style? Anything special?"

She nodded and scribbled as he answered the questions, the same list he had answered half-a-dozen times before. They talked about what he wanted, how soon he wanted to move, and his price range.

"Are you sure about this settling down thing, Ralph? I have a couple things that are real close to what you've bought before. Maybe you'd like to look at them before you make up your mind?"

She raised her hand, palm out, to stop his protest. "I have one or two in mind that fit what you've told me, too. Let me go through the listing book, see what else I can turn up, and then we'll schedule an afternoon—afternoons are still okay for you, aren't they?"

Ralph nodded. Once he was focused on business, he wasn't much for unnecessary words.

"Good. Then we'll schedule an afternoon to take a look at what I find."

Ralph looked relieved, almost as though he hadn't expected her to take his request seriously. "That sounds good. How soon can we get started?" He glanced at his watch.

Marty wondered if he really thought they'd run out and start looking in the next fifteen minutes. Ralph was sometimes impatient, but today's schedule was already crowded.

"Hang on. I have some calls to make this morning, and two listing appointments later today. I'll work on this in between. If you're really anxious, I'll try to get some things set up for tomorrow afternoon. Will that be soon enough for you?"

She smiled, hoping it would take any sting out of her words. She didn't want to put off a good customer, one who had also become a good friend, but she had already promised enough of her time to other people today.

"I guess." Ralph hung his head in mock despair. Then he raised his eyes to hers and grinned slyly. "But you know how I hate to wait for anything. Especially once I've made up my mind. You can make up for it by having dinner with me tonight."

Marty had expected the invitation, they had dinner regularly. But she was oddly relieved that she had an excuse this

27

time. "Not tonight, Ralph. I promised Lorraine we'd play tennis after work. Then there's a zoning commission meeting, and I drew the short straw this time."

Someone from the agency attended all the regular zoning and planning commissions' meetings, and it really was Marty's turn. Although trading was an accepted practice, she preferred to save favors for something more important than a casual, spur-of-the-moment, dinner invitation.

Seeing Ralph's look of genuine disappointment, Marty felt a pang of guilt, and relented a bit. "I am free for lunch tomorrow, if you'd like. We can meet here at twelve-thirty, if that works for you. I can fill you in over lunch, before we start the grand tour."

Ralph smiled. Somehow, it looked oddly shy. Ralph Gordon wasn't a shy man, but he was sure acting strange. "That'd be great, Marty. Willie's Grill all right with you?"

"Only if we go Dutch, Ralph. Even for lunch, that's spendy." She didn't feel right accepting lunch at one of the most expensive spots in town, but she cringed to think what the tab would do to her dwindling bank account. Still, she had to keep up appearances.

"Not a chance, darlin'. It'll be my treat. But if you feel better about it, we can settle for Ambrosia instead. Will that satisfy your pride?"

Marty had the good grace to blush. Ralph knew she lived on commissions, he knew that August was usually a dead month in a college town like Eugene, and he could figure out that she was skimping right now. He was dead right about her pride.

"Now, Marty," he continued, "before you say anything more, let me explain something. I've had some good luck in the last few months, and I want to celebrate. Besides, you'll more than make up for it in the time and effort you'll have to spend finding me a new house."

He put a finger to his lips, shushing her protest. "You'll get a commission, sure, but you work damned hard for me. I just want you to know you're appreciated."

It was a long speech for Ralph, and slightly out of character. They were friends, had been for years now. Why was he explaining all this?

"You win." Marty laughed, with an undercurrent of relief. If Ralph really had had some good luck, as he put it, he could afford the lunch. And she really would put extra effort into his search for a house. Repeat customers were a rare treasure in her business. Besides, she truly liked Ralph, and she tried to take good care of him.

"Fine. See you here at twelve-thirty." Ralph levered himself out of the chair, waved to her and hurried out the front door.

Chapter 4

Marty spent the afternoon, between appointments, checking the multiple-listing book, and calling agents she knew who might have something appropriate for Ralph Gordon. By the next morning, she had a list of possibles, and a couple of long-shots.

Ralph was almost a guarantee of a commission. He'd become a good friend over the course of many years, and she'd gotten used to his automatic passes.

When she was being honest with herself, she realized that Ralph was good for her ego. He made her feel attractive and desirable, but he took her turn-downs with good humor and didn't press her for more than she was willing to give.

When she was being brutally honest, she knew Ralph's infrequent attentions were enough to keep her from looking at other men. She didn't want to date anyone, but at least Ralph's attempts assured her that she could.

Today's lunch was a case in point. She didn't consider it a date, it was a business appointment. Nevertheless, she had spent more time than usual on her hair and makeup this morning. She was wearing a lightweight linen suit, in a shade of pink that complemented her pale complexion and highlighted her red hair. Her matching pink pumps were an inch higher than she usually wore in the office, and the top button of her silk blouse was undone, displaying a delicate gold teddy bear charm on a slender chain around her neck.

All right, so maybe she *did* care what Ralph thought of her. She liked Ralph, maybe even loved him as one loves an adorable older brother. But she wasn't in love with him.

Still, his openly admiring stare would lift her spirits and make her heart beat a little faster. It was exciting, in a nice, safe way that never threatened to upset her carefully controlled life. And she definitely wasn't interested in anyone that might upset the peace she had worked so hard to achieve.

She had her list of four possible houses, and the two additional, less likely, prospects. Looking at the addresses, she plotted a course that would put the two weakest places in the middle. With Ralph she had learned to save the best for last.

Will was sitting at his desk, trying to untangle an intricate web of contractors and schedules, when the phone rang. Eager for an excuse to put aside the tedious chore, he grabbed the receiver before Rita, his office manager, could reach it.

"Will Hart."

"Will, hi, it's George. Got a minute?" George always asked the same question, each time he called.

"Yes. Please!"

Will heard George laugh. "Seriously, George. I need a break, so you called at the right time. What can I do for you?"

"It's more what I can do for you," George answered. "I had a call from someone at Home Masters about the Bakers' house."

"You did?" Will could hardly believe his luck. "They have an offer?"

"Hardly. It seems there was a 'handyman' at the house a few days ago, who yelled at a couple and their agent. She was convinced they were going to make an offer, but he blew it for her." George's voice was dry, with a faint touch of sarcasm. "You wouldn't have any idea what that's about, would you?"

Will winced at the memory of his temper tantrum. "There wasn't supposed to be anybody there that day."

"Well, there clearly was, wasn't there?" George laughed again. "So what happened?"

Will gave him an abbreviated version of his dousing, and finished with an embarrassed laugh. "I figured it was no big deal, but it sounds like it was. I apologize for putting you on the spot like that."

George was chuckling when he replied. "No problem. It was worth it, just for the picture of what you must have looked like." His voice turned serious as he continued. "But she had some pretty good ideas about what might make the place show better, and I think you ought to consider them."

Will reached for a pad and pencil, and pulled them over in front of him, ready to take notes. "Shoot," he said.

Dependable as ever, Ralph showed up on the dot of twelve-thirty. They walked the three blocks to Ambrosia, Marty's heels tapping quickly along the sidewalk to keep up with Ralph's long strides.

The restaurant was cool, after the heat of the street. Marty blinked, her eyes adjusting to the relative darkness. The scent of rich sauces reached her nose—marinara and alfredo were specialties of the house—and her stomach growled.

The hostess seated them and took their order for iced tea. Then she gave Ralph a questioning look, and he nodded slightly.

A few minutes later, as they were ordering, the hostess returned. She carried a large package wrapped in elegant embossed silver gift paper, and tied with a shimmering pearlescent ribbon. She handed the package to Ralph with a smile.

Ralph smiled back, and continued ordering. The hostess retreated, and the waitress quickly followed.

Ralph set the package on the table, sliding away the wine glasses and maroon linen napkins folded into fan shapes. He pushed the package toward Marty.

"For you," he said. "With my thanks and appreciation."

Marty stared at the package, then at Ralph, then back at the package. Gifts from clients weren't unheard of, but Ralph wasn't your usual client, and she wasn't sure what strings might be attached to this gift.

"I'm not sure I should accept this," she said.

"Nonsense," he said. "There's no reason not to take a gift of thanks." He pushed the package closer to her, as she frowned at him. "You could at least open it before you tell me you can't accept it."

Still frowning, Marty reached for the package. She set it squarely in front of her, and stared at it for a minute. She was sure she looked as though she expected it to explode.

Finally, she tugged the soft bow, realizing as it untied that it was a gossamer scarf. Slowly she pulled the tape from the paper, and unfolded the wrapping, uncovering a box from the best luggage store in town.

She opened her mouth to protest, but Ralph waved a deprecatory hand at her. "Don't start in again, Marty. Just look before you make up your mind."

All right, it was only fair. She would take a look inside first. Then she would insist the gift was too expensive, and make him take it back.

She set the shiny paper aside, and lifted the lid off the box.

Inside was a briefcase of exquisitely colored tapestry, with dark brown leather corners tipped in polished brass. The handle was dark brown, and the latches and fittings were polished brass. Altogether a beautiful, and expensive case.

Marty was searching for a polite way to refuse when the waitress arrived with steaming plates. She set the box on the seat of the booth next to her to make room for her penne alfredo, with peppers and sun-dried tomatoes.

Before she could begin her protests again, Ralph insisted on hearing about the houses they would see that afternoon. As they discussed the various properties, he explained to her why he was celebrating.

"Do you remember that first place you sold me, up on Washington?"

How could she forget? It had been one of the hardest sales of her first year. She nodded.

"Did you know that I turned it into a bed and breakfast eighteen months ago?"

Marty shook her head. Keeping track of residential sales and development was a full-time job. She didn't pay much attention to the commercial side.

"I didn't really expect you would," he said. "But I did, and it's been very successful, thanks to you."

Marty swallowed a bite of pasta, and took a sip of water. "You don't owe your success to me, Ralph. Whatever you've done, it's been your own hard work. And you should be congratulated for it."

Ralph reached for the bread basket, and tore off a piece of the soft Italian bread. He buttered it, and chewed slowly. He was stalling, and Marty would have to wait him out. Finally he placed his hands on either side of his plate, palms down, and looked levelly at her. "Don't sell yourself short, Marty. You're a damned good salesman, pardon me, salesperson, and I wouldn't have bought that place without your persistence. You knew it would work for me, and you were right.

"Now let's eat lunch, and then you're going to sell me another house, one where I can settle down."

His tone didn't leave much room for argument. Marty decided to leave it alone. For now. "Okay, Ralph. Truce. Let's finish lunch so we can see those houses."

Through the rest of the meal, Marty and Ralph discussed the pros and cons of the various properties she had found. Finally, with a contented sigh, Ralph pushed his plate away. He patted his expansive middle, and chuckled.

"I'd forgotten how good this was. But I'm so full I'm ready for a nap." He pulled a piece of gold-colored plastic from his wallet, and laid it atop the check.

The waitress returned quickly, carrying Ralph's charge slip on a small plastic tray. Marty looked politely away while he added in the tip and signed the receipt.

She gazed around the crowded dining room, then stopped abruptly at the sight of a head of dark, curly hair. The man turned slightly in his seat, and Marty let out the breath she hadn't realized she was holding. It wasn't the handyman, but it had looked enough like him to give her a start.

She was relieved at first, but then she wondered if this was going to continue. Would she go along seeing him everywhere she went, whether he was there or not? No, she certainly wouldn't. It was just the shock of his behavior, and her call to George Lane that had her thinking about him. It would pass.

"Marty?" Ralph's voice brought her attention back to him. "Are you ready to go?"

"Sorry, Ralph," she said. "I just got a little distracted there for a minute." She glanced at her watch, and gathered up her purse and jacket. "We better get going, if we want to see the places I've got lined up."

Pointedly, Ralph looked at the briefcase, still laying on the seat where she had been sitting. She followed his gaze, and shifted uncomfortably. Unable to stall any longer, she picked up the box. Ralph took it from her, tucking it easily under his arm. They walked back the few blocks to the office in silence.

Once inside the office, Ralph placed the box on her credenza. She got the keys to the Lincoln she used for showing properties, and they went out to the car. Only then did she realize that she hadn't returned the briefcase to Ralph. She would, though, as soon as they were finished today.

Marty drove easily through the late summer afternoon. The intense heat of the previous week had momentarily given way to milder weather, though the sun was still strong.

At Ralph's suggestion, she lowered the power windows and turned off the air conditioning. The warm breeze felt good against her skin, though her hair tossed in the wind. Ralph reached in his pocket, and handed her the gossamer scarf that had been tied around her gift.

"Got in my pocket somehow," he said. "Maybe you can use it."

Unable to protest—she *did* need to cover her hair—Marty accepted the scarf and took advantage of a red light to tie it around her hair, corralling the red curls that had escaped her loose bun. Ralph nodded his approval.

They drove north, past the Beltline that had circled the city years before, when it was much smaller. Marty had noticed the listings of a couple new homes that fit Ralph's supposed requirements. Privately, she didn't think it was really what he wanted, but she had promised to show him what he asked for.

As she suspected, neither house met with his approval: the lots were too small for the large houses, offering little outdoor space, nor much privacy.

They headed back south. Marty stopped at a vacant tract house that had recently been renovated. Ralph walked through the house with her, but once more she knew it wasn't for him.

The renovations weren't his, and he found fault with nearly all of them. She wondered if Ralph really wanted what he'd said he wanted, or if he just *thought* he did.

Back in the car again, they drove past the fourth house, the weakest candidate in Marty's mind. Her judgment was confirmed when Ralph didn't even bother to get out of the car before telling her the house was wrong. She started the engine and pulled back into traffic.

"There are a couple nice places on the south side," she said, turning that direction. "One of them is way out near the community college, the other is just south of the university. I figured we could look at both of them, then I'll take you back to your car."

Driving through the university area, Marty couldn't resist taking the turn onto Agate, and driving past the house she had shown the Hortons. It was just curiosity, she told herself. She just wanted to know if anything had been done about the things she had told the receptionist.

The sight of the beat-up van in the driveway jolted her. She was sure it was the same van, and that would mean *he* was there. Her heart pounding, she speeded up, and went past without trying to see anything more, though she caught herself checking the rearview mirror after she passed.

"There was a sign on the lawn of that place," Ralph said. "Is it the one you wanted to show me?"

"No," Marty said, her voice strained. "Just a place I looked at the other day. I think it'd be perfect for you, but you keep telling me you're out of the renovation business, and this one needs a lot of work." She turned the corner, and stopped halfway down the next block. "This is it."

Ralph climbed from the passenger side of the car, and looked around. It was an older neighborhood, quiet and peaceful, with well-tended lawns.

"Nice area," he said. "The kind of neighborhood I had in mind, actually."

But the house didn't quite measure up. Despite the claims in the listing, it needed a roof, and the back porch listed suspiciously. Wearily, Ralph and Marty climbed back in the car. Marty started the engine.

"Say, darlin', how about we call it quits for today?" Ralph sounded tired, and Marty couldn't blame him. The warm breeze had died, and the sky had darkened ominously, promising a summer rainstorm. As though trying to outrun the coming downpour, traffic was thickening.

Glancing at the clogged intersections and sluggish knots of cars creeping along the main streets, Marty was inclined to agree. "Okay with me, Ralph. We're running a little late to see this last one, anyway." She darted down a side street, and headed back to the office, skirting the congested main streets.

"But let's re-schedule for early next week. I'll try to find some others in the meantime, and I still think you might like this last one."

Ralph nodded. "I just might, but I'm not sure I want to be that far out of town. I'm a city boy, you know. Not comfortable somewhere without street lights."

Marty laughed, her spirits lifting again. "All right. Let's get back and check the schedule for next week."

Chapter 5

Wednesday mornings were staff meetings at the Home Masters office. Marty arrived ten minutes early, snagging a cup of coffee to jump-start her day before she had to sit through the most boring hour of the week.

It was always the same: a pep talk from the sales manager, a lecture from the accounting manager about internal paperwork and controlling costs, some words of wisdom from the senior partner—who hadn't made an actual direct sale in fifteen years—a day-old doughnut, and back to work. If the goal was team-building, she had to admit it had some merit; by the time the meeting was over, the entire staff was united in their boredom and their antipathy for the senior management.

As they gathered in the grandly-named conference room, the sales staff murmured good mornings, and chatted in low tones about plans for the Labor Day weekend, just a few days away.

Gradually they settled into the cold, hard, metal folding chairs that were crowded around the imitation-walnut-grained plastic table. Though it was only nine a.m., the room was already over-warm, thanks to the dozen or so bodies packed into it, and the temperature was predicted to climb quickly in the late summer heat.

Lorraine took her position as class clown to heart. As she took her seat, she fanned herself. "Y'all know," she drawled, though she hadn't lived south of San Francisco in thirty years, "that I may dissolve before this meetin' does."

The crew chuckled.

The laughter died down as the management team entered the room. These few minutes were the only time in the week that the office was actually quiet.

Mr. Masters, the senior partner, led the group. Summer and winter he invariably showed up in a dark suit, striped tie, white shirt, and wing-tips wearing a shine that reminded everyone he was a retired Marine who knew how to spit-shine anything. His close-cropped gray hair and weathered face looked vaguely like Clint Eastwood—on a bad day. Jerry Masters wasn't a bad boss, but he had lost touch with the day-to-day operations. Nonetheless, he was a kind-hearted man, given to occasional fits of generosity.

Behind Jerry was Velma Little, the accounting manager. Dressed in a severe suit of pale blue silk with a cream-colored blouse, and her dark brown hair pulled high on her head, Velma looked cool and competent. In spite of the heat, and her stocky build, she would sail through the heat of the day without a wrinkle appearing, or a hair straying out of place.

Privately, Marty was of the opinion that even her hair and her suits were afraid to defy Velma's iron control. Jerry's occasional largesse made Velma crazy, and Marty could see a telling tightness to Velma's smile of greeting.

As Velma and Jerry took their seats, Ken Stocker, the sales manager, trotted in, panting. Ken had just passed his fortieth birthday, and he was determined to fight the aging process to at least a draw. He never drove when he could ride his bike, never rode the bike when he could walk, and never walked when he could run. He carried two boxes of doughnuts from the bakery down the block.

Ken's mocking grin told them he had, once again, lost the weekly argument of doughnuts versus fresh fruit for the morning sales meeting. He set the boxes on the table, then with a deliberate flourish he produced a bright green Granny Smith apple from a brown-paper supermarket bag. He had gone three blocks farther toward the university, stopped at the small organic grocery, bought the apple, and then run back to make the meeting on time.

If Ken weren't such a genuinely likable guy his stunt would have been offensive. As it was, it was just Ken's idea of irony. "Sugar time," he announced, biting into the apple as he took his seat.

Conversation sputtered to a stop, the doughnuts were passed, and they all settled down.

Ken spoke first. Setting his apple aside, he launched into an analysis of the quarterly sales and listings. "The numbers are down from last quarter, although they are above last year. I know the summer months can be bad, but school will be starting soon." He leaned forward, and they all echoed his movement. "Let's see if we can't get something moving in September."

Ken leaned back and picked up his apple again. Everyone straightened, and looked at Velma, who was next.

Velma gave them all a lecture about keeping their time sheets properly. Not that their hours mattered much. Commissions were what counted, and you didn't get them without putting in the hours. But Velma got excited by perfect paperwork.

Finally it was Jerry's turn.

Marty stole a surreptitious glance at her watch. Twenty minutes so far. If they were lucky, Jerry would be brief and they could get out of the room before the heat became unbearable, or one of them started snoring.

"Good morning," Jerry said, standing. He always stood to address his staff, though Ken and Velma had remained seated. "As Ken told you, we are anxious to increase listings and sales for the month of September, and in the coming quarter.

"However, the picture isn't quite as bleak as we have painted it. We had a busy spring, and the accountants called me this week with the projected earnings for the year, and they are pretty good.

"They told me I had to spend some money, and I could either give it to you, or give it to the tax man. I like you better." Jerry was usually willing to spend money, if it meant he could keep it from the tax man, who was his personal bogeyman.

He reached into the portfolio he had placed on the table in front of him, and pulled out a stack of papers. "Therefore, as a way of sharing our success, we are sponsoring a sales contest."

He handed the papers to Ken, who passed them around the table. "As you can see, there are levels of incentives, starting with the coffee mugs, dinner at the Electric Station, a weekend at the beach, and so on."

He paused for dramatic effect, watching as their reading caught up with his description. He resumed before anyone could reach the end of the page and turn it over. "The grand prize, if you'll look at the back of your sheets, is a seven-day Caribbean cruise for two."

A quiet chorus of approving comments greeted his announcement, punctuated by a loud "Awright!" from Craig Sailors.

Craig was a recent transplant from a much larger city,

where he had become accustomed to a more competitive atmosphere. Not a team player, Craig was suspected by many of the other sales staff of grabbing clients and cherry-picking sales leads. This contest was made for him and his tactics, and his fierce, possessive tone took much of the joy out of the morning for the others.

Marty wondered for about the hundredth time how much longer Jerry and Ken would tolerate Craig's antics.

She sighed quietly. That trip would be a wonderful thing, but she was afraid no one would be able to out-maneuver Craig.

Still, a seven-day cruise would certainly make it worth trying. Besides, it would be worth it, just to see Craig's face if someone beat him at his own game.

Jerry continued for a few minutes, giving them the groundrules, which were already carefully explained in the sheets they held in their hands. They were all glancing surreptitiously at the sheets in front of them, trying to pretend interest in what Jerry was saying, but it was clear that each of them was lost in a dream of blue seas and starry nights.

After another minute or two Jerry dismissed the meeting, and each of them scurried back to their desks, digging for client phone numbers and the multiple-listing books.

Marty scrambled through the next week, searching for another house for the Hortons, and one for Ralph. She was sure she could count on those two sales, if she could just find the right properties. She spent more hours in the office, taking ad calls, answering e-mail, and sending out relocation packets.

In the evenings she canvassed neighborhoods that seemed likely, looking for exclusive listings.

The neighborhood around the Agate house drew her back again and again. She drove past the house, and went door-to-door along the block where it sat, then repeated the process on the adjoining streets, and for three blocks each way.

She found one couple who listed with her, three more who listened politely, one extremely friendly yellow Labrador retriever, a noisy German shepherd, and a little girl who tried to talk her into adopting a kitten.

She wasn't sure why this contest had taken on such importance, but she was determined to at least make Craig work harder than he ever had if he wanted to win that cruise. And she wanted desperately to be the one to sell that house on Agate, if only to spite George Lane's handyman friend.

Each time she drove by the house, she searched the driveway for the white van, refusing to admit the disappointment she felt when it wasn't there. Once she thought she saw a sprinkler running, but she passed too quickly to be sure, and refused to go back to check.

Will stood across the street and looked at the Bakers' house, trying to be objective. Keeping his conversation with George in mind, he forced himself to strip away the pleasant haze of memories, and see the house as it was now, not the way it had been when he lived there.

The tiny porch looked forlorn in the bare front yard. Not like it had when Karen had planted flowers in the narrow beds around the foundation, and plants had hidden the sharp corners of the unadorned concrete porch.

It needed a new lawn, and fresh paint on the weathered trim. Both would have to wait until he could order paint and sod, and borrow a sod roller from one of his job sites.

But at least he could water, in the faint hope that something green would emerge.

And he could plant flowers. Somewhere, years ago, he had seen a house with trellised roses across the front. They had softened the blank front wall, and provided a splash of color. He thought it should work for the Bakers' house.

Will walked back across the street with a fresh perspective. Although he hated to admit it, he hadn't been seeing the house clearly. It had taken a stranger, a woman he had never seen before, to make him take an honest look.

He could do something about the outside right away. With a sprinkler running on low, he paced off the front and estimated what materials he would need.

He took a cheap spiral-bound notebook and pencil from his pocket, and scribbled a hasty note. He carried the notebook with him everywhere. It was a habit he developed when he was working for Paul Baker, and it had kept him from missing details on more jobs than he could remember.

Now he could afford whatever he wanted to make and store his notes on, but he stuck with his trusty notebook and a number two pencil. He didn't need fancy toys to shore up his self-image, and the simple notebook was a reminder of where he had come from. It was something he hoped he would never forget.

Sticking the notebook back in the pocket of his overalls, he checked the front door lock, and climbed into the truck. He would be back before the sprinkler needed moving.

Marty's efforts first paid off in the middle of September.

With the Hortons once again in tow, she had driven around the city, going back over the various neighborhoods.

After nearly an hour of seemingly-aimless wandering, chatting with them about each of the previous homes as she

46

drove past, Marty stopped in front of a new listing.

The conversation had reaffirmed everything she thought she knew about the Hortons, and it had put them in a good frame of mind. They were relaxed, ready to find the perfect house, and she knew what they wanted: a 1950s bungalow, like the Agate house, ready for them to move in.

From Mrs. Horton's smile at the front door, she knew she was right. By the time they were back in the office, the Hortons were planning where their furniture would go. They wrote up the offer, and it was immediately accepted.

Marty had actually scored the first sale of the contest.

Lorraine congratulated her good-naturedly, Ken gave her a grinning thumbs-up, and Craig scowled at her as though she had done him some great personal injury.

That Wednesday, when Ken presented the to-date sales figures at the weekly staff meeting, Marty was amazed to see that not only was she giving Craig a run for it, she was actually in the lead. The three listings she had developed gave her a slight edge, and one of them already had an offer. Unfortunately, the offer was from an ad call Craig had fielded, so she had to share that credit with him.

But she had another new buyer that had called her, and she thought the Agate house would be right for them. She called George Lane to make the appointment, her fingers crossed for luck.

Chapter 6

Will watched the construction crew while he talked to the foreman. He made a point of visiting every job site each morning and checking on the progress of each project.

When completed, the steel skeleton in front of him would be a new service center for an automobile dealer that had outgrown its current building. For now, it was a jumble of I-beams that didn't appear to have any pattern or plan.

But Will's practiced eye could see the building that would stand here in a few months. It was something he had always been able to do with industrial buildings. Now, it was something he was trying to learn to do with houses, or with one house, anyway.

Forcing the Bakers' house from his thoughts, he took a last look at the foreman's schedule.

There was a gap in the plan that could cost them several days. He pointed it out, and suggested a fix. The foreman's eyes widened as he realized his error, and he quickly amended the schedule, handing the clipboard to Will to initial the changes.

Will climbed back in his pickup, and drove back to his office. Strange how he could see the gaps and progress in a complex construction project, but the Bakers' house left him struggling for control.

Will was smart enough to know when he needed help. He was also smart enough to figure out where to find it. At the next stop light, he punched the speed dial on his cell phone, and got George Lane on the line.

"Can you set up a meeting for me with that woman from Home Masters?"

George hesitated, and Will continued. "I'd like to buy her lunch, an apology for screwing up her sale, and pick her brain about what else to do with the house. Think you can do that?"

"Probably. Let me get back to you later today."

"Thanks. I owe you one."

"And don't think I won't remember," George answered before he hung up.

Will left the pickup in the company lot, changed into his overalls, and grabbed the keys to the battered white van. The rose bushes should be in "will-call" at the nursery, and the trellises had been put up the day before.

Will loaded the roses into the van. Before he closed the back door, he stopped to take one more look around. He was thinking about the bare front porch, and what he could do to make it look a little better.

By the time he finally left the nursery, he had a selection of fall-blooming crocus and colchicum, salvia, sedum, and amethyst ajuga. He loaded the last of the plants in the back, but he hesitated before slamming the doors. He needed something with color right now. With the guidance of the nursery manager, he selected a couple large clay pots with late-blooming yellow mums.

The yard would look much better, even if his knees were already protesting the work to come.

★ ★ ★ ★ ★

Pulling up in front of the house, Marty was immediately struck by the changes. The lawn had obviously been watered regularly, and although it wasn't lush and beautiful, it had regained some color. But the biggest change was the rose bushes.

The roses were planted across the front of the house, at least six of them, with sturdy trellises behind them, rising to braces dropping from the gutters. The freshly-turned earth was dark brown, piled around the roots of the new plants. A few tentative branches had twisted up two of the trellises, giving a promise of lush greenery and fragrant blossoms in the spring.

With a start of unexpected excitement, Marty realized that the van was in the driveway again. Still, she groaned inwardly, wondering what kind of lunatic behavior would greet her this time. Dreading the encounter, she ushered her clients through the unlocked front door, and began the walk-through of the now-familiar house.

They stood in the hall outside the master bedroom, discussing the kind of changes she felt would make this a "dream house." She could hear rustling noises in the dining room, but tried her best to ignore it. They would have to face His Rudeness soon enough.

Then again, maybe George Lane had warned his seller. With luck, the handyman just might be on good behavior while there were prospective buyers in the house.

When they turned the corner into the dining alcove, however, her hopes shattered like crystal goblets against a fireplace. He was there all right, in faded jeans and a close-fitting T-shirt, surrounded by water trays, glue brushes, knives, and rollers. He was wallpapering the dining room. If he kept this up, the listing would certainly have to be changed from "fixer-upper."

In any case, he was scowling at them as they came into the room. It was the only expression he seemed capable of in this house.

"Could you give me a hand here?" he said to Marty, indicating a roll of wallpaper that appeared ready to tumble across the floor. He softened his mouth into a polite smile that didn't quite reach his eyes, though it did improve his expression. A little.

"Please?" he said, his tone a few degrees warmer.

Marty realized he was trying to be pleasant, and it was obvious that he really did need help. Smiling coolly in return, she stooped down and retrieved the errant roll of paper. She handed it to him, and he curled the excess around a broom handle.

Marty felt a jolt of electricity pass through her as their hands brushed, and she immediately felt the heat of a blush creeping up her neck and across her cheeks. Her creamy redhead complexion had always given her away when she was surprised or embarrassed, often compounding the problem by calling attention to her.

"Thanks," his clear gray eyes strayed ever so briefly to her left hand, "Miss—?"

"Ms. Francis," she supplied, stressing the non-specific title. After blushing like a schoolgirl, she certainly didn't want to give him any more information about her. "You're welcome. Now, if you'll excuse us, we'd like to finish looking at the house."

She was curious about what he was doing, but didn't want to appear ignorant in front of her buyers. She led them through the kitchen, then out to the unadorned concrete slab that had defined "patio" in the era when the house was built.

"The back yard hasn't had much done with it, but in some ways that's a real plus. In so many houses of this vintage there's a lot of bad 'improvements' you have to remove before you can begin to make it your own."

She pointed out a few other things, and continued her pitch as they came back through the kitchen and dining room, though she was sure by now that the handyman and his apparent ineptitude at papering had once again cost her the sale.

"That back yard is much larger than most in this area. There's plenty of room to enlarge the master bedroom and bathroom, or add many of the things you've told me you wanted. I know that's what I'd do if this was my house."

What in the world was she saying? She was not the least bit interested in buying a new house, much less one that needed as much work as this one did.

But the idea of improving the house *did* interest her, to her surprise. She wasn't sure if it was the challenge of making the house live up to its potential, or something else. She just knew that this house had a hold on her, and she wanted to find it an owner.

She headed for the front door, waving a vague good-by to the handyman as she went.

Marty had never met George Lane, though they knew many of the same people. She was surprised when he called her.

"Ms. Francis? George Lane. I'm the listing agent on the Agate house, the one you've been showing? I was hoping you might do me a favor."

"That depends," she said, "on what it is you need."

"It's really pretty simple. I don't normally deal in residentials. My usual work is in institutional investment portfolios, but I do have a broker's license. I only took the listing on that place as a favor for a friend, and he's concerned because it isn't moving."

"It does need some work," she said. She was reluctant to criticize too harshly. After all, the owner was a friend of George's, and there was no need to antagonize a stranger unnecessarily.

"I suppose it does. We listed it as a fixer, but there seems to be a lot of market resistance. I know you've shown it a few times, sort of taken an interest in the place. Will, Will Hart, that's my friend, thought you might have some ideas, since you've been showing it, and he asked if I could arrange a meeting for him."

Marty rolled her eyes, but she held her tongue. Lorraine raised a questioning eyebrow across the office, but Marty shook her head silently. She didn't need anyone to run interference on this, at least not yet. "Certainly, George. I'd be glad to do it. When would Mr. Hart like to meet me at my office?"

"Actually, he wouldn't. He said since he was taking your valuable time, the least he could do was compensate you somehow, and he suggested he buy you lunch."

Lunch? She wished Will, George's dear friend, would simply call her on the phone. There was no need to eat up an entire lunch hour with this. But it probably wouldn't hurt to have someone like George Lane owing her a favor.

"I suppose that can be arranged. Let me take a look at my calendar." She pulled her calendar from the battered brown leather briefcase and looked at her appointments for the next few days. "Do you know what days are good for Mr. Hart?"

"Fridays are usually pretty good, or any day if you can make it a little later, say, one-thirty or two. He did say that he would work around your schedule."

At length, she agreed to meet Mr. Hart at Francisco's at one-thirty on Thursday. She wrote the appointment in her date book, and slipped it back in the briefcase.

Ralph's extravagant tapestry gift, still in the box, was sitting unused underneath her credenza. Although she had taken it back to the office, she didn't feel comfortable using it, and she hadn't found a graceful way of returning it yet.

She really liked Ralph, and didn't want to hurt his feelings, even though the gift was far too extravagant. And she didn't want to offend him while he was still looking for a new house. She wanted to help Ralph find the perfect house, and, to be honest, she wanted the sale.

With that in mind, she went back to scanning the day's new listings, making a list of possible properties for Ralph. She scribbled a note to herself to make a stop at the Agate house on Thursday morning before meeting Mr. Hart for lunch. It would be a good idea to have it fresh in her mind.

Maybe she could get Ralph to go with her. It would be one way of getting him to look at the house, under the guise of asking his opinion about what she should recommend to the owner. Even if he wasn't interested, he had a lot of experience with renovations, and he would give her good advice.

Chapter 7

Watching Ralph walk through the Agate house, Marty could see he was taking an interest in the project. They started, as she always did, in the bedrooms at the end of the hall. Ralph took in each room with a practiced glance that caught more than most people would with a lengthy inspection.

The weather had turned cool and gray, a precursor of the rain and fog to come as summer yielded to autumn. They flipped on lights in the hallway and the bedrooms, but it still felt small and dark.

"First thing I'd do," Ralph said, "is get some more light in here. Maybe start with the master bedroom. Bump that back wall out about eight feet, enlarge the bathroom, and put in a lot of glass on the back wall."

He pulled the heavy, short drapes aside, to illustrate his point. The weak light penetrated a short ways into the room, but the small windows limited its effect. "Maybe some sliders, so you'd have access to the back yard."

"I was thinking along those lines, though maybe not that elaborate. But I don't know if I'd recommend it to the seller. It sounds like a lot of work for a house you're trying to unload."

"True, but from what you've told me, this place is

under-priced. With a little creative financing, he could do the work, and recover the costs on the back end. If he doesn't want to go that far, he should at least consider just replacing the windows with sliders. That would accomplish much the same thing, except for the space. But if you can use the back yard as an extension of the room, it'll seem a lot bigger."

"Great idea, Ralph. I like the sliders, and I'll take your word for it that they could be done with a minimum of cost."

Ralph thumped the wall under and over the windows experimentally. "I think the wall is solid enough to take it. Might need to raise a header over the doors, but the biggest expense will be the doors themselves. I'd suggest storm windows, if he'll go for them. That lets him keep the drapes open during the cold weather."

They continued through the house, inspecting things as they went. Marty had been pretty sure Ralph would like it, but she was surprised at how enthusiastic he was.

Inspecting the new wallpaper in the dining room, Ralph turned to her and grinned. "You know this is why I keep coming back to you. You always manage to find something that intrigues me. You like this house a lot, don't you?"

She peered out the dining room window, at the forlorn-looking patio slab. "I don't know if I *like* it Ralph. I feel like there's an incredible potential for this place, like it could be just the perfect house for someone, done up right." She dropped the corner of the curtain back over the window. "But it is someplace I *could* like. Does that make any sense?"

Ralph chuckled as he headed toward the kitchen. "Absolutely. You've just described how I feel about it. I keep telling you we're made for each other."

Marty laughed. "Sure we are. But you'd get bored with me just as fast as you get bored with your houses. No thanks."

Ralph pretended to pout. It was like a kind of game with him. He had to try, and she had to brush him off. Marty didn't want to become romantically involved with anyone, especially Ralph.

But she remembered the electric jolt when she had handed the wallpaper roll back to the handyman, and a faint heat rose in her cheeks. It was just static electricity, she told herself.

"I wouldn't get bored, not with you," Ralph said. Then with a slight leer he added, "There certainly isn't anything about you that needs remodeling."

Now Marty blushed in earnest. "Honestly Ralph." She laughed. "Don't you ever give up?"

"Nope. But I do have work to do this morning. I'm sorry to have to cut this short, but I've got to get going. Thanks for showing me this place, darlin'."

He shoved himself away from the kitchen counter where he had been leaning. "Just find me a place like this, but with all the work done, and you'll have yourself a deal." He blew her a kiss, and went out to his car.

Marty heard him drive off. She should do the same, there were other clients who needed her attention, but Ralph had been right. She did like this house. It could be fixed up to be bright, cheerful, and comfortable.

Still, she wasn't the one looking to settle down. No more than she already had, and certainly not with Ralph. She felt a great deal of affection for him, and they were good friends, but it would never be more than that.

It might never be more than that with anyone, but she was content. She had her house, a quiet and comfortable life, and a job she loved. Her life was the way she wanted it. So why did she need to keep reminding herself of that fact?

She went out onto the porch, and took a look at the nearby houses. The neighborhood was one of those older, established kind of places, where neighbors knew each other, and people sat on the front porch in the evening. It was the kind of place where you might raise a couple kids.

That thought shattered her calm. Where did kids come from? Was that a biological clock she heard ticking in the background? Certainly she was too young to worry about that. She had a lot of years before she had to decide about any of it.

She shook her shoulders, telling herself it was just a macabre fantasy, brought on by Ralph's passes and the gray drizzly weather.

Carefully locking the house behind her, Marty hopped in her car without looking back, and headed for the office. She'd turn her thoughts into a brief note to the owner, present it to him over lunch, and make her exit as quickly as she could without being rude. Then she'd forget this house and get back to the paying customers.

At least until she found the perfect owner for the house. She promised herself she wouldn't be back until then.

Chapter 8

When Marty entered Francisco's, the weekday lunch crowd was thinning, and most of the tables were unoccupied, though not yet cleared. The hostess looked at her expectantly, asking, "Just one?"

Marty swallowed her irritation. She resented the suggestion in the woman's tone that there was something wrong with a woman eating alone. It was an attitude she'd seen before, and she knew she'd see it again, but it never failed to irritate her.

"Actually, I'm meeting someone." She glanced at her watch. It was one-thirty exactly. "I'm not sure if he's here yet." She realized that the description George Lane had given her wasn't much help in identifying her lunch partner.

"Mr. Hart?" she asked. Marty nodded. "He's expecting you. Just follow me, please."

The hostess led her to a small table near the back of the restaurant, where a dark-haired man sat with his back to them. As they approached, he turned and stood up. He extended his right hand, and she automatically met it, her mind spinning and a blush creeping up her neck.

"Ms. Francis. How nice to see you again." He shook her hand warmly, leading her to a chair. He released her hand and pulled the chair back for her. "Thank you so much for coming. I appreciate you allowing me to make this imposition on your time."

Marty sat, grateful for the chair as her knees wobbled. Her hand tingled from the brief contact. She looked up into his clear gray eyes, stammering in her confusion. "You, you're Mr. Hart? George didn't tell me, I mean, I thought, that is, I didn't know you were the owner of the house."

Beneath the table, Marty clenched her hands into fists, fingernails digging into her palms. Her initial confusion had been replaced with a simmering anger that threatened to spill over. Her knees were shaking, and her stomach felt as though she had swallowed glass.

She forced herself to take a deep breath, as she fought for control.

His laugh was rich and deep. "Does it really matter? Actually, I was afraid you might not be willing to meet with me if you knew who I was. After all, our first encounter wasn't the best way to make friends and influence people."

She was surprised by his candor, but her surprise could not replace the hot flash of anger she had felt. He seemed to think a lunch and a little sweet talk would excuse his rude behavior.

She wanted to give him a piece of her mind. She would, too, as soon as she was sure she could be civil. But before she could formulate an appropriately pithy response, he said, "I owe you an apology for that. You had no way of knowing I had disconnected those pipes. I should have put a note on the sink, or something.

"I didn't know anyone would be showing the house—they weren't supposed to—but I should have realized someone could turn up unexpectedly. It was my own fault."

Marty hesitated. After all, he had behaved like a tyrant, then tricked her into lunch with him, and now he thought he could just say "I'm sorry" and it would all be forgotten. She didn't want a public scene, she hated to draw attention to herself, but she wasn't going to let him off that easy.

"You did take us by surprise, Mr. Hart. I thought maybe someone else was showing the house. Your timing certainly could have been a lot better. I'm afraid your reaction may have cost us a sale." She set her mouth in a prim line, neither forgiving nor overtly disapproving.

"I know," he said. "George told me that. That's why I wanted to talk to you. He says you're good, and you seem to have taken an interest in the house and the neighborhood."

Their conversation was interrupted by the waitress. Realizing she hadn't even looked at the menu, Marty asked for another minute, and hastily opened it and scanned the selections. The distraction gave her a chance to study Will Hart without being obvious.

The dark hair, which had been plastered to his head the first time she saw him, was fashionably short, above his collar, and neatly trimmed on the top and sides. There were the traces of gray at the temples that she had noticed in the Mexican restaurant, and a tiny streak on top. His gray eyes were clear and bright, brimming with intelligence and good humor.

He caught her gaze, making her avert her eyes in embarrassment, but not before she saw a grin highlight the fine laugh lines around his mouth and eyes. She decided on the spot that he didn't take himself too seriously after all. Nobody who grinned like that could.

After they ordered lunch and the waitress had delivered their coffee, Will tried again.

"Ms. Francis . . ."

"Please, just call me Marty. Everyone does."

"Okay, Marty. If you'll call me Will."

She nodded.

"Let me explain a couple things to you," he said. "Houses and real estate are not my usual line. I'm taking care of this place for some old friends who left the state suddenly because of a family emergency. I knew George. I asked him to take the listing as a favor to me, and suddenly here we both are, neither of us knowing near enough about what we're doing."

He paused while the waitress placed their salads in front of them, resuming as she walked away. "After your call, George figured maybe there was something to what you said, and did some checking, both on the house and on you. I suggested we talk to you, and he thought it was a good idea." He grinned, looking sheepish. "He wouldn't come, though. Told me I had to take the heat alone."

Marty nodded, chewing slowly. She wasn't sure what to make of this revelation. Surely George knew other residential agents. On the other hand, maybe no one else had taken an interest in the place. Or maybe he thought Will needed to make amends. Whatever the reason, she would take it at face value for now. If there was anything more to it, she was sure it would show up eventually.

"Mr. Hart—Will—I stopped by the house this morning and took another look at it. There are a couple things that will help, and that won't cost much. You've already helped by getting that front yard spruced up. A dead lawn makes the buyer think everything's been neglected, and then they're on the lookout for every hint of trouble, even if it isn't there."

She pulled the neatly typed sheet from her purse, and handed it to him. "These are a series of recommendations. What it amounts to is brightening up the place. Light-colored paint, replace the heavy drapes with light curtains or mini-blinds, that sort of thing. If you want to take on a little construction, I'd suggest you open the house up, and let more light in."

He studied the list as they ate, occasionally glancing up as though re-assessing her based on what he read. The silence stretched until Marty thought perhaps he had got what he came for, and she could excuse herself and get back to the office. She set her napkin aside, as Will spoke.

"I appreciate what you've done here. Very professional, very businesslike. But I want something else." He paused. "You *like* that house, don't you?"

She nodded. What was it he was getting at?

"You like it, but there are some things that you'd do if it was yours, right? I don't think those things are in this memo."

She sat very still. This was not at all what she was expecting. Why was he asking her these things? "I tried to make suggestions based on the anticipated return, not on what I personally would like. I know what appeals to me, but that isn't necessarily what appeals to buyers."

"Nonsense. Right now you're the top seller in your office, and you're consistently in the top two or three. Your taste and your opinions are extremely valuable." He placed his hand over hers—that jolt again—and held her eyes with his.

"Truthfully, I owe these people a lot more than just getting their house sold, and if I can do something to get them a better price, I'd like to do it."

He moved his hand, idly stroking her fingers, seemingly unaware of the effect he was having on her. "Ten more minutes, Marty. It shouldn't take any longer than that."

She drew her hand away, covering the motion by using

both hands to dab at her mouth with her napkin. Every time she looked at those clear, gray eyes, she knew she would gladly stay there all day with him. This couldn't be happening, not to her. He was a client for heaven's sake, and there was probably a Mrs. Hart somewhere besides. But she could maintain her cool for just ten more minutes, while they finished eating lunch. He had admitted he was wrong, and apologized. Certainly his apology had earned him that much. It had nothing to do with the electricity that coursed through her at his touch.

Ten minutes stretched to twenty, as she described the cosmetic and then the structural changes that she would make. She explained about opening up the master bedroom, letting in more light, using the back yard to make the house itself feel larger. She stopped suddenly and looked at him intently.

"I'm getting carried away here. If you did all the things I've been talking about, it would mean practically rebuilding the entire house. Not a very good way to spend your money."

"If it makes the house the best it can be, it certainly *is* a good way to spend my money." He seemed amused at her sudden backpedaling. "Besides, I can do a lot of this stuff myself. I put myself through college working summers on construction crews. It's been kind of fun to get back into it."

He certainly looked capable of manual labor, his chest broad, shoulders straining ever-so-slightly in his custom-fitted sports coat. But it was clear he was no longer accustomed to it. The hand that had laid atop hers was soft and warm, not heavily callused, and the nails were clean and lightly buffed.

"Well . . ." she drew the word out, giving herself time to think. "Of course you can do whatever you want. But the bottom line is that bathrooms and kitchens give back the best return on investment. As long as it's within reason," she added hastily. "I mean, it's a nice neighborhood, but if you overbuild you'll never get anywhere near your initial investment returned."

"Bathrooms and kitchens. I'll keep that in mind, I promise. But I really like the idea of putting sliders in place of the windows in the back. I think I might try to do something about that."

Marty glanced at her watch, surprised that her lunch had stretched to nearly two hours. Talking with Will was so easy and comfortable, but it wasn't getting her job done. She had better get back to concentrating on her real work.

"You need to go." He made it a statement, not a question, as though he had read her mind. "I'm talking your ear off, and taking you away from your work, and I promised not to take too much time. I hope you'll forgive me. My enthusiasm for this project seems to get the better of me sometimes."

His sincerity melted Marty's reserve. She *did* have to go, but that didn't mean she couldn't help; he really seemed set on doing something with the house. Besides, she told herself, this really is your work. If he fixes the place up, you'll have a better chance of selling it, and get a better price. Better price, better commission. Just business.

She knew she was rationalizing what she was about to do, but she did it anyway.

"Thanks so much for lunch, Mr.—Will." She smiled in what she hoped was a warm-yet-professional manner. "If there is anything else I can do for you, please call me."

She presented him with her business card, adding almost defiantly, "My home number is written on the back."

She turned quickly, pulling the strap of her handbag over

her shoulder, and hurried from the restaurant, before he could reply. She knew she was blushing furiously, and if anyone noticed or called attention to it, she'd get even redder and more embarrassed.

She could hardly believe she had done something so forward. What was this effect he was having on her? She *never* gave any clients her home number, preferring her calls to go through the answering service, and certainly not someone she knew so little about as she did Will.

After all, what did she really know about him? He had deep gray eyes, sometimes soft and amused, sometimes holding a quick intelligence. His hands were strong, yet soft against her own. She found herself wondering what his hands would feel like on other parts of her. She stopped that line of thought before it could go any farther. There was no need of adolescent fantasies about a man she hardly knew. Nothing could come of it anyway, so why continue?

Still, his firm shoulders and broad chest were inviting, the kind of place any woman would want to rest her head. On his shoulder, Marty? she asked herself. He's at least a foot taller than you. You'd rest your head against his stomach, like some little kid leaning on daddy. She had to stop this foolishness.

And what about Mrs. Hart and the little Harts? If she gave him a wife and children, that ought to pour enough cold water on her fantasies to squelch them. She could just make them up, the way Beth told her she made things up anyway.

Squaring her shoulders, she walked the remaining blocks to the office, enjoying the warmth of the late-September sunshine. In a few days or weeks the sun would disappear behind the cloud cover of fall, so she'd enjoy it while she could. And she would *not* think of Will.

Will watched Marty hurry away from the table and bolt out the front door of the restaurant. Her face had flamed when she handed him her card, and he had stifled the impulse to chuckle. It wouldn't have been polite, and he had just finished apologizing for his rude behavior.

The last thing he wanted to do was offend *Ms.* Marty Francis once again. Telling her she was cute when she blushed would not have been well received, he was sure, even though she was cute.

He'd always had a thing for redheads, although Karen had been a brunette. Karen. Working on the Bakers' house had brought back memories he thought had been long buried. The way they had buried Karen. It had happened so fast, before they had time to build a life together.

Instead, he had channeled his energy into building a successful business, one that left little time for intimate personal relationships. But he hadn't been able to dismiss the shock he had felt when he had touched Marty's hand as she handed him the wallpaper.

He had tried to discount the feeling. It could have been a lot of things, none of them important. He had reached for her hand today, as a test. He told himself he would feel nothing, and he could go on about his business with that problem cleared up.

Instead, he had felt the same electricity, the same connection, that he'd felt before. It surprised him, and he didn't know what he wanted to do about it.

She had tried to disguise it, but she had clearly pulled away from his touch. He wondered what she was afraid of, but he wasn't sure he wanted to find out. He didn't have room in his life for the kind of complications that Ms. Marty Francis represented.

Chapter 9

When she arrived at the office, everything was in an uproar. Craig was in Jerry Masters' private office, along with Jerry, Velma, and Ken. Dotty, the day-time receptionist was in there, too, and the door, usually standing open, was firmly closed.

Marty couldn't see much except Dotty's face, her eyes red-rimmed and streaks of dark mascara running unheeded down her cheeks. Whatever was up, it didn't look like good news for anyone concerned.

Marty grabbed a cup of coffee, went to her desk, and sat down, trying not to stare at the single window to Jerry's office. She could see that Jerry had gotten up from his chair, and was pacing, or as close as he could get to pacing, in the crowded room.

He would move two or three steps in one direction, then turn and move back the other way. His hands were clasped behind his back, his head thrust forward, like a bulldog straining at his leash.

Marty didn't think she had ever seen Jerry this visibly upset, even when his daughter had eloped with the University of Oregon starting fullback. Jerry was a basketball fan.

Trying to look casual, Marty lifted her phone and dialed Lorraine's extension. Lorraine was at her desk, trying to ap-

pear deeply absorbed in the latest issue of the multiple-
listing book, and failing utterly. She picked up the ringing
telephone, and gave her name, carefully avoiding looking at
Marty.

Before Lorraine could finish her greeting, Marty spoke.
"So, what in the hell is going on? You go out for a simple
client lunch, and when you come back, the receptionist is
bawling her eyes out and the boss looks like he's about to
have an aneurysm. If this is what happens, I may never dare
to go to lunch again."

"I'm not real sure." Lorraine looked down at her desk,
and pretended to make notes. "I was at lunch myself when
Jerry came in. He went in his office and was in there when I
got back. That was weird by itself, since he's never in the
office in the afternoons."

Marty nodded, still avoiding looking at Lorraine. Jerry
was usually on the golf course by one o'clock, unless it was
pouring rain. "Go on."

"Well, then Velma goes in there with some printout from
her precious computer." Velma's possessive love of the accounting computer was an office joke.

"Anyway, they talked for a few minutes, then Velma
comes out and asks Diane to cover the phones 'for just a
couple minutes,' and she asks Dotty to come in. Next thing
you know, Dotty's in tears, Ken comes back from a lunch
meeting with Craig, both of them looking like they'd eaten
ground glass, they all go in there, and bam! The door
closes, and that's about the time you came in.

"I have never seen Jerry look that pissed," Lorraine continued. "Even when his daughter—"

"—eloped with the fullback," Marty finished for her.
"Neither have I. And I can't imagine what it is." But she
could imagine, only too well. She hoped she was wrong,

that it wasn't the usual, tawdry office affair. Oh, how she hoped she was wrong.

Craig was married, though that hadn't stopped him from making a pass at anything in a skirt, including Marty herself.

But it was Dotty she worried about. Dotty had a husband and the sweetest little boy, barely a year old. Things had been tough for them in the last few months, what with Dotty's husband being out of work, but Marty just didn't think she was the type to find comfort in the arms of a sleazy character like Craig.

"I can imagine," Lorraine said, "but I don't like any of the ideas I've come up with. Not that I give a damn what happens to Craig, he's such a creep, but I wonder what Dotty has to do with any of it. She's such a good kid, and I hate the idea that she's mixed up with him some way."

A shout from Jerry's office made them both jump guiltily. Craig was on his feet, and yelling at the assembled group in the office. Lorraine quickly whispered, "Later," and cradled the phone. A few seconds later, Marty followed suit.

No one noticed.

They were all openly staring at the office, where Craig continued to yell. He turned to the door, yanking it open with a violent jerk. His face was contorted with anger, as he yelled back over his shoulder, "Who wants to work with this bunch of losers, anyway?"

Without waiting for an answer, he stomped dramatically to his desk, grabbing his monogrammed rosewood nameplate and ebony pen and pencil set.

He threw them into his open briefcase, slammed the lid, snapped the locks, and yanked it off the desk.

His dramatic exit was marred by the fact that his elegant,

pure silk designer tie had caught in one of the clasps, and he did a good imitation of a whiplash victim when the force of his yank on the briefcase nearly dislocated his neck. Holding the briefcase awkwardly in front of him, he hurried through the front door, and into the street. Angry horns and squealing tires marked his progress as he jaywalked to his Miata, parked at the opposite curb.

Lorraine caught Marty's eye across the office, and they both shrugged. Who knew what was going on? But whatever it was, if it meant Craig was gone for good, it was ultimately going to be good news.

Everyone in the office tried to busy themselves with pushing papers around their desks. After another fifteen minutes, Jerry emerged from his office, his arm protectively around Dotty. Velma, her eyes fierce, and Ken, his face an impassive mask, stood behind them.

All eyes swiveled to Jerry, who cleared his throat and waited for silence. Velma sidled over to Diana, and asked her to switch the calls to the service temporarily, a sure sign of Big News.

Silence quickly followed, as phones stopped ringing, calls were hastily concluded, and conversation ceased.

Jerry looked from one to another of them, and sighed. "I'm sorry that you all had to be treated to Mr. Sailor's childish display. We found some disturbing trends in our records, and this is the result of our attempt to discuss them with the parties involved.

"Dotty, did you want to say something?"

The young blond nodded, as tears threatened to spill over again. She blinked furiously, then started talking in a tremulous, breathy voice. "I owe you all a huge apology. I'm very ashamed of what I did. I hope you will all be able to forgive me someday."

The remorse was so clear, the guilt and shame written so plainly across her face, that everyone's sympathy was immediately engaged. She sniffled, then continued.

As she spoke her voice grew steadier and stronger, the purging power of confession giving her strength. "I've been helping Craig. He found out about my money problems, and he promised he would help me out, if he could just win the sales contest." She winced at the shameful memory. "He said it wasn't much, I just had to let him have his 'fair share' of the ad calls, even if he wasn't in the office when they came in. Just make sure he got what he kept calling 'a fair shake' when the clients called.

"It didn't seem like a lot, and he was sure he wasn't getting his share of the calls because he was new."

She shook her head. "I can't explain it, but the way he said it, it made sense at the time." She looked up at Jerry, understanding spreading across her face, like the sun rising after a stormy night.

"Jerry, it wasn't the money, I really don't think it was. I think he just wanted to prove that he was better than everybody else, even if he had to cheat to do it. He never talked about the money, only about how he'd be the best, about how he'd beat everybody."

Jerry patted Dotty's shoulder paternally. She really was just a young kid. "Dotty," he said kindly, "why don't you take the rest of the day off? We can talk about the rest of this tomorrow. Okay?"

Dotty nodded tiredly. The confrontation in Jerry's office, and her public apology, had taken all her usual starch out of her. She quickly gathered up her purse and jacket from the reception desk, and started for the front door.

Marty's heart went out to her. She was sure Dotty expected to be fired any minute, and she knew, too, that her paycheck was the only thing between her little family and the street.

Without making a conscious decision, Marty walked briskly from the spot by her desk to the front door. Leaning her red head close to the drooping blond one, she put her arm around Dotty and squeezed her shoulders. She put her mouth near Dotty's ear and whispered, "Don't worry, it'll all work out okay. You'll see."

Lorraine joined her for a moment, backing up Marty's assertion that it would work out. Between the two of them, they got Dotty out the door with something of her usual strength and resilience restored, then rejoined the staff grouped around Jerry, Velma, and Ken.

It was Ken who spoke this time. His face seemed longer than usual, and his normal cheerful attitude was gone. Marty remembered he had been the one who had hired Craig, and had been his defender in his early days.

"Craig was engaged in some unethical practices, and his association with the firm has been terminated, effective immediately. We also suspect some misrepresentations in his expense accounts. Velma and I will clear his desk of personal effects, and see that they are delivered to him.

"If anyone asks, you are to simply say that he is seeking career opportunities elsewhere. If it's a client, offer to help them. If it's other business, refer it to me, or Velma. Any other calls should go directly to Jerry." He stopped, as though considering his next words very carefully.

"This will have a decided impact on the sales contest. Craig was currently the number one salesperson. We have not yet decided what to do about his sales and listing credits. When we do, we'll let you all know. We will try to be as fair as we can to all of you."

He looked down at his hands, then looked up, and met

the eyes of each of them in turn. "I would also like to apologize for bringing Craig into this firm. He had me fooled, and I don't think I fool easily. I hope I have learned something from all of this."

The impromptu meeting dissolved into little knots of conversation. Jerry left by the front door, Velma in his wake, muttering something about a meeting with the company attorney. Lorraine sidled over to Marty, barely suppressing a grin. "Well, at least we're rid of ol' Craigy-babes. I sure won't miss the unwanted fingerprints on my anatomy. But what a mess for Dotty.

"And what came over you? You're usually the one reserving judgment, waiting to consider all the viewpoints, doing all those careful, judicious things, and here you are throwing your arms around her and telling her it'll be okay. What gives?"

Marty shifted uncomfortably. She didn't know exactly why she had responded to Dotty, but it had seemed right at the time. "I don't know. Craig was just such a creep, and Dotty's just a kid, a scared kid with an out-of-work husband and a baby to support. I couldn't bear to see her so completely crushed."

"Good for you." Lorraine gave Marty a thumbs-up gesture, then her eyes widened. "Brace yourself, here comes some more complications." Marty turned to find herself face-to-face with Ken. He smiled tentatively.

"I hope I'm not intruding, but I do need to ask you a favor. Craig was scheduled to cover the planning commission next Monday, and he obviously won't be there. Can I get you to cover it, Marty?"

She quickly reviewed her plans for the coming week. "Can we change tennis to Tuesday, Lorraine?"

When Lorraine nodded, Marty turned back to Ken.

"Sure. I'm glad to help you out."

Ken's relief was obvious, and his slight grin was genuine. "Thanks, Marty. You're a lifesaver. It's good to know that there are people you can count on in a crisis." He turned to go, then turned back, looking sheepish. "Can I ask you two something, please?"

They nodded, though Marty had some misgivings.

"We still have to decide what to do about Dotty. I'm not sure what's the best approach. I admit I'm worried about her loyalty to the firm, if she could do something like this. But she also told us about her financial problems, which none of us knew about. That made her vulnerable to Craig's manipulation. I guess what I want to know is how you two feel about Dotty."

Marty hesitated, then looked squarely at Ken. "She made a mistake. Eventually, it might be better for her to find another job. But she's admitted her part in this, and faced all of us, and apologized. That's a lot more than Craig had the guts to do. I say we keep her on, at least until we can make the change as gracefully and painlessly as possible. For everyone."

Lorraine nodded in agreement. Ken thanked them for their help, thanked Marty again for covering the planning commission, and continued around the office, apparently taking a straw poll on the Dotty issue.

From the expressions of the people he talked to, Marty had a hunch that Dotty's job was safe for now.

Chapter 10

Will swung the heavy sledgehammer. It hit the wall with a bone-jarring crunch, and plaster dust flew into the air. He smiled to himself. There was something intensely satisfying about the physical labor of demolition.

George Lane coughed as the dust reached his throat, and Will glanced over. "I told you to wear a mask," he said, his voice muffled by the blue filter held over his mouth and nose by an elastic band.

George shook his head, unable to speak. His hand was clamped over his mouth, and his eyes were covered by safety goggles. With a resigned shrug, he grabbed a mask and pulled it over his face.

"Makes it hard to breathe," George grumbled through the mask.

"Easier than breathing plaster dust," Will answered, pulling the hammer back for another swing.

Another two blows, and laths broke, revealing framing members. The electrical wiring had already been disconnected, and the window removed. A temporary brace supported the wall over the window. All that remained was to remove the wall itself, and make it ready for the sliding glass doors.

George stepped around the bracing that held up the

wall, and gathered an armload of broken laths. He put them in a trash can, already half full of debris, and glanced over at Will.

"Want me to take a turn at that?" He gestured at the heavy sledge, hanging from Will's right hand.

"No." Will gritted his teeth and took another swing. Each time the hammer hit the wall, the impact ran up his arms and through him. It felt good.

He had to admit, though, that wielding the sledge was tiring. He was too warm, and the mask didn't help. He laid the sledge down and walked out of the room, gesturing for George to follow him.

Safely away from the plaster dust, Will stripped off the mask. He grabbed a can of the soda they'd stashed in the refrigerator, and handed one to George. A cold beer would taste good about now, but not while he was handling anything more powerful than a screwdriver.

"She got to you, didn't she?"

Will glanced at George. He could pretend he didn't know what he was talking about, but he knew it wouldn't do any good. George had known him too long.

"What do you mean, 'got to me'?" He took a long swallow of soda, watching George from the corner of his eye.

"I mean, you're taking everything she said to heart." George gestured down the hall, where a thin layer of dust had settled over the carpet. "We're knocking down a wall! That's a little more than fixing up the place, I'd say."

"She said I could get a better price, and I believe her. You told me she was one of the best, so I take her advice. It's important to me. I just want to do right by John and Betty, that's all." Will knew he sounded defensive.

The dust had settled down, and George headed back

down the hall to the master bedroom. With a shrug, Will followed him hoping he would let the topic drop.

Not likely.

Standing in the empty room, looking at the exposed bones of the house, George looked thoughtful. "How long were you and Karen here?" he asked, as though he didn't already know the answer as well as Will did.

"Fourteen months. Senior year, and the summer after. You know that."

"Yeah, I know it. But do you? You moved out the week of her accident, and I'd bet you haven't been back since."

"So what? Karen died. I moved. End of story." Will pulled the mask back over his face, and picked up the sledge. Without checking to see if George's face was covered, he pulled the hammer back and blasted the wall again.

The weekend was Marty's busiest time. Out-of-town prospects came visiting, she held open houses at some of her listings, and she showed up early on Sunday to field ad calls from early-risers. It was, she assured herself, what made her a good salesperson, and gave her the edge she needed to win that Caribbean cruise. She wasn't in the lead right now, but she knew she could win.

Maybe, she thought, she was as bad as Craig, wanting to prove she was the best. But she'd do it by working hard, by putting in the extra hours, by doing her homework, and by knowing what her clients needed. She didn't need to cheat to win, and she would prove it.

This weekend started off well. She got a call from Mr. and Mrs. Beatty, a couple who had been referred to her by the Hortons. They didn't think they were ready to buy, just yet, but they wanted to start looking.

Marty silently congratulated herself on the African violets she had sent Mrs. Horton for her new kitchen. Mrs. Beatty made a point of telling her how thoughtful it had been for her to send such a sweet gift.

Marty spent nearly an hour with the Beattys on Saturday, talking with them about their needs. Early on Sunday, they called her back. There was a listing that sounded perfect for them in the morning's paper. Could she take them right over? Marty agreed to meet them at the office.

When she arrived at the office, Marty quickly checked over the ad the Beattys had called about. She could hardly believe what she found. The Beattys wanted to see the house on Agate.

She didn't understand why the ad was even running, what with Will's determination to continue with his do-it-yourself home improvements. But there it was in the classifieds, and she had promised to take the Beattys over that afternoon.

She called the listing office for an appointment, and crossed her fingers. There was no telling what she might find when she got there.

Driving over, she kept the conversation light. They discussed the change in the weather, and all agreed that it was getting colder at night, and fall certainly was in the air.

Mr. Beatty asked her opinion of the university's football team, and then launched into a five-minute monologue detailing his reasons why they couldn't take the conference this year. His preference for the Arizona State Sun Devils was based on careful statistical analysis. Also on the fact that his son had gone to school there.

When they arrived, Marty tried to tell herself she was relieved to find that the white Dodge van wasn't in the driveway, as it had been on her previous visits. But underneath her relief there was a stab of disappointment.

She realized she had been excited at the prospect of showing the house to the Beattys, if only on the chance that she might get to see Will. But the house was locked tight, and there was no sign of anyone else around.

As she walked through the front door, Marty felt a chill, as though a cool breeze was blowing through the living room. There was a draft somewhere.

She would call Will tomorrow and remind him to light the furnace, and to check that draft. A little heat would improve the chances of selling. It would be strictly a business call, nothing more.

She led the Beattys down the hall, past the two small bedrooms and the bathroom, and into the master bedroom.

She was ready to start her pitch, when she stopped in the middle of the room and stared at the back wall. More precisely, she stared at where the back wall used to be. Now she knew why the house was so cold.

True to his word, Will had taken her advice. But he had taken it to extremes that Marty couldn't have imagined when they had had lunch just a few days before.

The back wall of the bedroom was gone, as was the wall between the bedroom and the bathroom.

On closer examination, she realized that the back wall was only partially missing, but there was a huge hole cut in the remaining portion. A sheet of clear, heavy plastic covered the cut-out and the missing section of wall adjoining the bathroom.

Through the plastic, she could see rough foundation work, extending from the bathroom about six feet into the back yard. A hammer, level, and assorted tools she couldn't immediately identify were scattered across the bathroom counter, now obviously being used as a carpenter's bench for the current project. There was a coiled extension cord in one corner of the room, and Marty spotted a Craftsman circular saw case.

She turned to face the Beattys, stunned at the destruction she had just encountered.

"As the listing says, this is a fixer-upper." She scrambled for an explanation, *anything* to ease the shock evident on their faces. "There aren't any major *repairs* to do, but it needs some sprucing up, and some brightening. I believe that the windows in this room are being replaced with sliding doors."

She gestured toward the distorted view of the yard through the wrinkled plastic sheet. "Just imagine how lovely the view will be when the doors are in place. They will give you direct access to the back yard."

It wasn't a very good pitch, but she was trying to recover as gracefully as she could. "Let's take a look at the rest of the house. I'm sure you'll like it."

Marty gave them her best smile, but she realized that no matter what she said, this sale was a goner. She could find the Beattys a house, but they sure weren't impressed with this one. Still, though she did her best to present the house in a positive light, she cut it short, forced to acknowledge the growing disinterest on the part of the Beattys.

She didn't want them to think she was a complete fool, and based on her initial performance, they just might.

"I apologize for the mess in the master bedroom. I had no idea they would get so carried away," she said, widening her eyes into an earnest expression. It was a trick she found worked well with older couples.

In the back of her mind, she was kicking Will around the block for blowing another sale. This house was quickly moving from being a personal challenge to being an albatross she couldn't rid herself of.

This house and that man.

She carefully hid her thoughts of revenge, and watched the fatherly concern grow in Mr. Beatty's expression. He'd give her another chance, and her impression was that Mr. Beatty was the decision-maker in this family. To clinch it, she gave him another reason to forgive her.

"I'm going to call the listing agent when I get back to the office, and tell him about what we found here. It certainly makes the ad you read sound very misleading, almost as though they were trying to lure you in, then sell you something more expensive." She was pretty sure the real cause was simple ignorance, but she wanted to put the Beattys and her on the same side of any potential conflict.

She followed the Beattys out to her car, carefully locking the door behind her. She didn't think it really necessary, since there was a gaping hole in the back of the house, but years of training had her double-checking the lock box to satisfy herself it was properly secured.

She climbed into the driver's seat of the Lincoln the agency leased for chauffeuring clients, and started the engine. She hesitated before pulling away from the curb to let a white van pass her. But, instead of driving past, the van slowed, then turned into the driveway.

She recognized it instantly, and gunned the car into the street, leaving a startled-looking Will standing in the driveway, his arm half-raised in a cheery greeting.

For the next hour, Marty drove the Beattys around Eugene, showing them any listed houses that she suspected they might find interesting. They were all occupied, but there were three they showed an interest in. She let them out at their car, promising to call them the next afternoon to schedule a tour.

She considered what she should do next. Will had definitely seen her before she pulled away from the house, and she knew from the perplexed look on his face and his upraised arm that he had recognized her, and expected her to greet him. It was better that she hadn't, but she still was tempted to drive back over, just to see if he was still there, and give him a piece of her mind.

This was the third time his handyman antics had cost her a sale, and, as they say, the third time's a charm. She'd show him charm, if she got close right now. The Beattys, like the Hortons, and the Murrays of the dining room wallpaper incident, would take extra time and care to salvage what should have been a sure sale.

George's dear friend Will was costing her time, and time for Marty was money. Deciding that her bad humor had been suppressed for long enough, she headed for home. A hot shower, a little ice cream, and a couple chapters of the latest Tony Hillerman murder mystery were the antidote she prescribed.

Maybe she could rename the victim in *this* book Will.

Chapter 11

Marty walked through her front door, carrying a Food Value grocery sack. The market had been out of her way, but it was the only place in town that carried Danken's ice cream. It came from a little shop in Seattle, and she considered it far superior to anything else she had ever eaten. And today was definitely a day for a top-of-the-line indulgence. She'd earned it.

But before she could get the carton open, the telephone started ringing. She ignored it, taking a delicate china bowl from the cupboard. Only her best china was good enough for the way she felt today.

She was rattling in the silverware drawer for an ice cream scoop when she heard the answering machine pick up the call.

Her recorded voice came from the other room, asking the caller, in her most polite tones, to "Please leave your name and number after the tone, and I will call you back as soon as I can."

Fat chance today, she thought. I am in no mood to talk to anybody about anything. Whoever it was could just wait until tomorrow. All the anger and frustration of the afternoon was boiling up, demanding she pay attention to it.

The machine beeped, and a vaguely familiar baritone replied. She cocked her head to listen, then she heard the name "Will", and realized it was him. It was just too much.

After she had stayed away from him, avoiding the confrontation, bottling her anger until she got home—after all that, he had the gall to call her at home. Well, he was going to get an earful, and now was as good a time as any.

". . . buy you dinner tomorrow?" Will was saying to the recorder as she grabbed the phone and punched the Power Off button.

"What do you want?" she demanded.

"Wha—? Marty, is that you? I didn't think you were home. Boy am I glad I caught you."

"Really?" Sarcasm dripped from her voice. "And why is that, Mr. Fixit?"

"Oh." His voice dropped from a cheerful rush to quiet and reserved. A silence dragged on. After a minute, he said softly, "You're angry with me, aren't you?"

"Angry?" Marty's voice grew louder. "Angry? Why should I be angry with you? Is there something I should be angry about? Like maybe the fact that I just got sand-bagged, *again,* on that damned house."

She hesitated, shocked that she was swearing at a man she hardly knew, but her indignation carried her on. "Like having to grovel at the feet of a nice, older couple, apologizing for the mess that place is in? Like having to explain that some idiot who doesn't know what he's doing has cut a giant hole in the back wall, and is playing carpenter? Is that what you mean?"

Marty was shaking. She didn't like yelling at people, didn't like the display of uncontrolled emotions, and it wasn't something she did very often, and never to people with whom she did business. Always proper and polite, that was her attitude. Always in control.

On the other end of the phone, Will was quiet.

Oh geez, she thought, I've really done it this time. I have messed this up big time, and when Jerry heard about it—and she was sure he *would* hear about it—she would have to eat a lot of crow. Forget winning any sales contest. She'd settle for keeping her job.

She was already composing the letter of apology she knew Jerry would demand, as he had demanded of other agents who had been out of line with clients, when she heard Will chuckle.

Just what did he think was funny about this? But she wouldn't ask, she'd let him have his fun. She didn't want to make things any worse for herself than they already were. She gritted her teeth and waited for him to speak.

The chuckle continued for a few seconds. When he finally spoke, his tone was apologetic. "I guess maybe you've got a right to be mad. But you sure have the temper to go with that hair, don't you?"

The wonder in his voice was too much for Marty. She couldn't stay mad with anyone for very long, and she had to admit that she'd let her stereotypical redhead temper flare in a way that few people had ever seen. She started to giggle.

"Marty? Are you okay?"

She giggled again. "Yeah, I was angry, but I never have been able to *stay* angry. That's the real secret about redheads, you know. One flash, and then it's over. I guess I really owe you an apology for flying off the handle like that." Maybe Jerry wouldn't have to hear about this after all, if she could smooth this over with Will.

"No harm done. And you don't need to apologize. I can see where this must be frustrating as all hell from your standpoint. But that isn't why I called you."

"Oh?" She kept her voice carefully neutral, afraid to even guess what he *had* called for. She waited.

"Like I told your machine, I called to see if you were free to have dinner with me tomorrow night. I promise we won't even have to think about the house, if you don't want," he added hastily.

"I don't know, Will. Let me check my calendar."

Marty was stalling. She laid down the receiver, and rummaged in her purse. She knew she had promised Ken she would cover the planning commission meeting, and she should just tell Will she was busy. It was the truth, and it was what she had told Ralph just a few weeks earlier. But she wanted a minute or two to consider the invitation.

She spotted her address book on her desk, and rifled through the pages, mentally listing the people she could get to cover the meeting for her. There were at least three other agents who owed her big favors.

She picked up the phone again, and tried to act nonchalant. "I think I can make it tomorrow night. Depends on the time though. Things are a little disrupted in the office this week, and I may end up having to stay a bit late." There, that would give him a chance to back out gracefully. But she hoped he wouldn't take the opportunity.

He didn't. They agreed on seven-thirty, and he arranged to pick her up at the office. Dinner would be all right, but she still wanted the freedom of having her own car nearby. It would make getting home a lot less of a problem. Always better to keep her options open.

When she hung up, Marty realized that she had nervous flutters in the pit of her stomach. Not only had she agreed to have dinner with Will, but she had accepted a date, a real date, one she couldn't even pretend was related to her job. After all, he had said they wouldn't even talk about the house if she didn't want to.

She had no desire to get involved with anyone, especially someone she did business with. Dating simply wasn't a part of her life right now. Not after Charlie. It had taken three years to put her life back together, and she didn't want a man, any man, to disturb the peace she had finally found. And on top of that, she would have to find someone to cover the planning commission meeting before six o'clock tomorrow.

She sat down at her desk, pulled the address book toward her, and picked up the receiver. It was time to call in a few favors.

Chapter 12

"So," Beth said, "tell me about this guy you're having dinner with." She looked so smug, Marty had to wonder for an instant whether she had anything to do with it. She dismissed the thought as impossible, but Beth kept up her chatter.

"It's about time you started dating again. I kept telling you Charlie isn't worth this."

The two women were eating fast-food tacos. Beth had called when a client had canceled a tour of a Christmas tree farm, due to rain and mud, and Marty had been glad to join her for a quick lunch.

They watched the steady crawl of traffic through the gray drizzle running down the brightly painted front windows of the downtown Taco Bell.

Now Marty wasn't so sure having lunch with Beth had been a good idea. Not after she let slip her dinner plans with Will.

"There isn't much to tell," she shrugged. "He's a friend of George Lane, and I've been helping him with a house he wants to sell. George doesn't keep up with the residential market, and he asked if I'd talk to this guy. So I talked to him, and he wanted to have dinner."

"Not much to tell." Beth's disbelief was clear. "You

haven't so much as seen a man after dark since you and Charlie split up. Of course there's something to tell. What does he look like? How old is he? Is he married? Divorced?"

"To tell the truth, I don't know how old he is, or if he's married, or anything else about him. He caused me some problems a couple times showing this house, and I think dinner is his way of trying to make up for that."

Her voice dropped to a puzzled whisper. "For all I know, I'll get there and find myself having dinner with him and his wife, or his girlfriend, or maybe even his *boy*friend. Wouldn't that be a lovely way to spend an evening?"

Marty grimaced and pushed away her half-finished taco. She sat with her head lowered, staring at the table. Marty seemed to do that a lot. She could feel Beth studying her, and she could well imagine the familiar look of concern in Beth's eyes.

Beth reached across, and tilted Marty's face up to look her in the eye. "Hey," she said softly. "You're really interested in this guy, aren't you? C'mon, tell Auntie Beth all about it."

"That's the worst of it, Beth. There really *isn't* much to tell. We had a very proper business lunch, and I thought that was all there was to it. Then he shows up at that house again, making a mess with his repairs, again, and I'm acting like a stupid teenager! Next thing I know, I'm—"

"Hold it." Beth's eyes narrowed. "Is this the plumbing guy? The one you said was such an arrogant jerk? The hunk we saw in Los Baez that night?" Her voice went up an octave. "Is *that* who you're having dinner with?"

Marty nodded. Even without Beth putting it all together like that, it all seemed too much. And when Beth strung it all out like that, it was just too absurd to think about. As foolish as she felt under Beth's questioning, she did see the

90

inherent silliness of the situation. She laughed, in spite of herself.

"Yup. Can you believe it? I hardly know the guy, I know next to nothing about him, but I not only agreed to have dinner with him, I rearranged my schedule and called in a favor to cover a meeting I was supposed to attend. Me, who wore her wedding ring for a year and a half to discourage guys from even talking to me."

Her expression grew more serious. "But, Beth, there's something about him. I don't know exactly what it is, but he makes my stomach get all fluttery when he looks at me, and each time he's touched my hand it felt like I had hold of a live electric wire. It's like a magnet pulling me in, and I'm so scared of what I might find . . ." Her voice trailed off once more.

"What you might find," Beth said gently, "is that you're still a woman. You've spent the last three years pretending you weren't, trying to be invulnerable, trying not to have feelings. You keep telling yourself that if you don't let anyone close, you can't get hurt. But if you don't let anyone close, you are going to miss out on a lot of good things, too." She patted Marty's hand.

"Find out if he's married first, that's just being reasonable. If he is, get him out of your life, pronto. Nobody needs a man like that, including his wife. Especially his wife. But if he's available, well, just relax and enjoy the fluttery parts."

Marty worked through the afternoon in a fog. Fred had agreed to cover the planning commission meeting—he owed her for covering for him on his daughter's second birthday—and she had the rest of her work under control. There were two deals pending, and she made follow-up calls, checking on financing details, inspections, and the like. As long as she kept busy with details, she didn't have to think about her plans for the evening.

As dusk crept across the front windows, the office began to empty. Dotty, tentative but still employed, left at five. Velma closed down the computer and left about five-thirty, with Ken right behind her. By six, it was just Marty and Fred, and he was packing up to meet his wife for a quick dinner before the planning commission meeting. Soon, he too was gone.

Marty locked the front door behind Fred, and returned to her desk. She tried to concentrate on the reading she had on her desk—a variety of newspaper and magazine articles on market trends and population patterns. But she couldn't keep her mind on the work.

As she read about average family size, she imagined herself with one-point-eight children. Would that be one child, or two? What if she wanted *more* than two children? Did that make her above or below average?

She shoved the thought of children aside, and turned to an article on housing prices. But the figures for median housing prices in the local market started her thinking about the house on Agate, and how it fit into the current statistics. What would happen to it when Will finished the master bedroom project he was doing? She wandered off into yet another fantasy, living in the house with her dream man and their children.

After fighting her fantasies for three-quarters of an hour, she gave up, slammed the file folders shut in disgust, and carried her makeup case into the bathroom. She wouldn't need fifteen minutes to fix her hair and touch up her makeup, but it was better than sitting at her desk, mooning around like some lovesick adolescent. How could she think any of this about Will? She didn't know anything about him, including whether there was a Mrs. Will, besides the one she had made up after their first lunch together. Staring at her face in the mirror, she was startled to realize that in her thoughts he had become "Will" instead of "Mr. Hart" sometime in the last week.

She was reading so much into a simple dinner invitation. She knew it, and she vowed to stop it immediately. Beth would tell her she was making things up, and that she needed to get out more often. Beth was right.

She would forget all this baloney, comb her hair, fix her face, and go enjoy dinner . . . whether or not there was a Mrs. Will along for the evening.

Chapter 13

Will arrived five minutes early, while Marty was still fussing with her hair. She pulled her coppery hair back from her face, secured it with a pair of simple tortoise-shell combs, and allowed the curls to fall loose on her shoulders. She had decided it was a bit too flashy, and was about to tone down the look when she heard his rap at the front door of the office. Too late to change it now. She gave the combs a final tweak, straightened her shoulders, and smoothed the slim skirt of her dark green jersey dress. She was as ready as she was going to be.

Grabbing her purse as she went past her desk, she stopped at the front of the office to turn out the lights, and check that the phones were re-directed to the answering service. She pulled her camel's-hair coat from the coat tree, and belted it in snugly around her trim waist before opening the door. She locked it behind her and shook the handle to double-check.

When she turned around, Will was looking at her with undisguised appreciation. "You look great," he said. "I really like what you've done with your hair."

Marty was grateful for the dim lighting on the sidewalk, because she could feel the color creeping up her cheeks. How she hated the fact that she couldn't control her blushing.

"And," Will continued, "I like the way you blush when someone compliments you."

Her hand flew instinctively to her face, trying to cover the growing redness. He reached out and gently pulled her hand back down.

"Don't. It's nothing to hide. I said I liked the way you blush, and I do." Still holding her hand, he drew her along the sidewalk to a midnight-blue Plymouth sedan parked at the curb. He opened the door and helped her in, closing the door behind her. As he walked around to the driver's side, she marveled at the courtesy. It had been a long time since she'd been with a man that opened doors for her.

They drove in silence for a few minutes. Marty was nervous, not knowing what to say to this man. She hardly knew him. As the silence continued, she began to regret accepting the invitation. What had possessed her to accept a date with a total stranger, someone she knew next to nothing about? She had decided they would have to start with the weather, and the University of Oregon Ducks football team, when he spoke.

"I hope the Electric Station is all right with you. It's one of my favorite places."

"That's lovely." She didn't quite know how to react. The Electric Station was an elegant and expensive dinner house, very popular with the upscale business and social crowds.

On a weeknight there would be a small, somewhat noisy crowd in the bar, a few tables full of people in suits engaged in earnest conversation, and the occasional couple dressed up and celebrating some special occasion. She and Charlie had eaten there on their first anniversary. By their second they had eaten burgers in a coffee shop, and they hadn't bothered to make the pretense of celebrating the third. Still, the restaurant was a pleasant place, and she didn't carry any deep-seated feelings of regret.

Will had made reservations, and they were shown immediately to a quiet table in a secluded corner. Will took her coat, and held her chair for her. She smiled up at him in thanks.

They studied the menu for a moment, then, as if by agreement, both put them down at the same time. They busied themselves with the details of ordering drinks and dinner, and were finally settled at the table with their appetizers and beverages in front of them.

This is it, Marty thought. Now is when we stare at each other and wonder how we're ever going to get through the next hour or two without boring each other silly.

It had been years since she had been on a real date, and she was sure she'd completely forgotten how to behave. She tried to remember how it had been in high school, and later, but all she really remembered was being tongue-tied and awkward.

Will raised his wine glass. "A toast. To the prettiest real estate agent in town." He touched his glass to hers and sipped his Chablis, looking at her over the rim of the glass. Marty hesitated, then took a sip of her chardonnay. The smoky sweetness slid smoothly down her throat. She could feel the warmth in her empty stomach, and a spreading relaxation in her arms and legs. She would have to be careful she realized, since she was drinking on an empty stomach.

She reached to break off a piece of bread, deciding that some food was the best solution, just as Will did the same. Their hands touched, and she felt the same electric jolt she had before. She pulled her hand back, but Will captured it with his own, and held it tenderly in his for a moment before squeezing it lightly and releasing it. He pulled the bread from the basket, tearing a small slice free, and offered it to her. Flustered and unable to speak, she simply nodded. He placed the slice gently on her plate, and pushed the butter toward her. Only after he was sure she was served did he take a slice of bread for himself.

To cover her confusion, Marty spent a long time carefully buttering the bread, and passing the butter back across the table to Will, careful to avoid touching him. The simple touch of his hand had left her shaken, and she was afraid of how strong her reactions were.

She took a tiny bite of the warm, crusty bread, chewing slowly, and enjoying the combination of yeasty sourdough and sweet butter. She had another sip of wine, savoring the contrast of tastes, smells, and textures. She concentrated on the bread and wine, trying to ignore her growing awareness of Will, and how close he was. She knew if she looked up she would see his soft gray eyes, fringed with startlingly dark lashes, studying her. She wondered what he saw.

Did he see her as she really was? A confused thirty-two-year-old divorcee who hadn't had a date in three years, and who was starting to notice the first faint lines around her eyes? Could he see her awareness of the faint ticking of a biological clock? Did he see those first pale strands in the dark copper of her hair, the ones she carefully plucked out each time they appeared?

When she finally felt strong enough to face him, Marty raised her eyes from her plate and looked up at Will. He was sitting quietly, his hands resting lightly on the tabletop. In one hand he held the stem of his wineglass, idly running his thumb along the curve where the stem joined the base. To Marty the simple caress seemed somehow terribly intimate and sensual. She had to say something, to distract herself from these disturbing thoughts. She cleared her throat.

"Do you follow the Ducks?" she asked, starting with her first "safe" topic.

"I keep track of whatever makes the headlines, and I go to an occasional basketball game. But I'm not crazy about football. In fact, I'm not much of a sports fan. I know that's a terrible thing for a macho guy like me to admit." He grinned in a way that told her the macho reference was a joke. "But it's true. I like to play more than I like to watch, most of the time."

"What sports do you play?" Marty was surprised at how closely his attitude matched hers, and her curiosity helped her relax.

"Softball in the summer. Tennis when I can find a partner who plays down to my level. When the weather gets too bad to be outdoors, I play racquetball at a local club. But I don't like playing indoors near as much. How about you, are you a sports fan?"

"Not football, nor basketball. But baseball. I grew up with a father who was dedicated to the Cubs, and he taught me to love the game. Since there isn't a major league park in three hundred miles, I settle for a few minor league games during the summer." Daring herself to continue, she said, "And I certainly agree with you about playing instead of watching. I play tennis all year. The cost of a club through the winter is horrid, but it's one of my luxuries."

"Everyone should have a luxury or two. With some people it's cars, or houses, or clothes. Or tennis clubs in the winter," he grinned.

"What are your luxuries, Will?" His name felt funny on her tongue now, warm and personal, and all too good. She wanted to say his name over and over. She took a sip of wine, and focused back on the conversation, trying not to notice how his hair curled so perfectly over the tops of his ears.

"My luxuries?" He frowned slightly, and rubbed his chin. "Let me think about this. What do I indulge in?"

They sat in a comfortable, friendly silence for a couple minutes, but were quickly interrupted by the arrival of their salads.

For a while they were distracted by the waiter with freshly-ground black pepper, refills of their water glasses, checking their bread and wine. Finally they were left alone again. Marty poked at her salad, making sure there were no beets on the plate. She hated beets bleeding their deep red juices across her salad.

"No beets," Will said with a sigh of relief. Marty started at his voice.

"Did I say something about beets?" she asked. Maybe she had said something out loud without realizing it.

"No. *I* said, 'No beets.' I hate beets on my salad, and they seem to be all the rage lately. I forgot to ask them to leave them off, and I was worried there might be some. But why would you say anything about beets?" His brow furrowed in puzzlement.

"It was just weird. I was checking to be sure there weren't any beets, and then you said that. I thought maybe I had said something instead of just thinking it." She shook her head in embarrassment. "Never mind. It was just one of those strange coincidences, nothing important."

Will nodded, and took a bite of his salad. He smiled and nodded again, waving his fork toward the salad in a gesture that implied approval.

After a couple bites, Will looked up at Marty and grinned. "I know one of my luxuries: taking attractive women out for dinner. Not one I get to indulge nearly often enough."

Marty puzzled over his comment. She thought he meant

it as a compliment, but it made her worry about how many other "attractive women" he might take to dinner. She realized what she was feeling: jealousy.

"That's one luxury," she said evenly, controlling her emotions. "What others?"

"Let's see. Margaritas and salty tortilla chips when the weather's warm. Chocolate in any form." He stopped and laughed. Marty liked the sound of his laugh, solid and deep. It was a good laugh. "Listen to me. Everything I've come up with involves food. Now you know my deep, dark secret. I need all those tennis and racquetball games to work off the calories of all my luxuries!"

Marty laughed with him. "Food luxuries are the easy ones," she said. "I have *lots* of those, especially the ones that involve ice cream. But what else? Movies? Travel? Books?" She wanted to know everything there was to know about him, wanted him to tell her about his entire life between the salad and entree, about his family over the main course, and all his hopes and dreams with dessert.

"Movies, yes. Books, yes. I'd love to travel, but I don't have the time. I guess that would make it a real luxury, wouldn't it, if it's something I can't take the time to do. So I do most of my traveling through books and movies, seeing and reading about places I'd like to go someday. I don't watch much TV, though, because so much of it takes me places I either don't want to go, or places I've already been and I never want to go back to. But I've been talking about me all evening. Tell me about you." He held up his hand like a stop sign. "But not about your job, I know enough about that. I want to know *you,* what you like, what you do. All the little details like . . . are you married?"

Chapter 14

Had he really just asked her if she was married? Well, if she answered that, it would give her a chance to ask him the same thing. She swallowed, and plunged ahead, hoping her voice would stay steady.

"I'm divorced, actually. Three years." She waved her left hand airily. "Long enough for the tan lines from my rings to fade, along with the worst of my 'cynical divorcee' attitude." She had to do it now. Keeping her voice deliberately light, she asked. "How about you?"

"I was married for a short time right after college," he said. He hesitated, then seemed to come to a decision. He looked squarely at Marty. "She died in a car accident just after our first anniversary."

"I'm so sorry." Marty was instantly sorry for the flippant tone in which she had asked the question. She reached out and covered Will's hand with her own. The electricity was there, but underneath it there was a warmth and comfort she hadn't felt before.

"You don't need to be sorry, Marty." But he didn't move his hand. Instead, he turned his hand over and held hers. He spoke in a low voice. "We had a good thing while it lasted, and it was a long time ago. I try to remember only the good things, and let the rest of it go. For a long time I regretted so many things—all the things we planned to do and didn't have time for, the children we never had, lots of stupid things. But I learned many years ago to focus on the things we *did* have."

Marty sat silently, letting Will hold her hand, wanting him to go on holding her hand. After a moment he continued in a cheerier tone. "So now I'm what is loosely termed 'an eligible bachelor.' Though I wish I knew exactly what it is I'm eligible for."

Marty rewarded the attempt at a joke with a smile. He had obviously said more than he had intended, and was trying to cover an awkward moment with humor. He squeezed her hand and let it go, fussing with the bread basket and his salad plate.

"I don't know quite why I went into all that, but you just looked so stricken when I told you Karen had died. I was afraid I had done something to upset you."

"No, no." Marty hurried to reassure him. "I just had been joking and teasing, kind of, and then you said that and it felt so insensitive. But I'm glad you told me, really." She smiled.

The intense moment passed, and Marty's embarrassment eased.

Over dinner they compared books and movies they had enjoyed, finding a common interest in mystery novels, and each admitting to finding action-adventure movies an occasional 'guilty pleasure.' Marty confessed her passion for ice cream, and they talked about where each had gone to college, and the jobs they had held. Talking of summer jobs brought them back to the subject of construction work, and to the house on Agate.

"The thing is," Will said, "I'm finding out I really like fooling around with a hammer and saw again after all these years. I'm a little out of practice, and some of the things I start turn out to be harder than I remember, but it's been kind of a fun challenge."

He shook his head and gave her a self-depreciating grin. "The wallpaper probably should have been a two-man job, but I managed it. It just took about three days longer than it should have."

"You did look a little frazzled the day we were there. It seemed like there were buckets and brushes and knives everywhere, and the wallpaper was definitely not cooperating."

Will laughed ruefully. "It wasn't one of my best moments. Thanks for rescuing me."

"Anytime. Amateur wallpaperers rescued, day and night, low rates. Call now, operators are standing by."

Will laughed again, a strong, happy sound. "You really have a great sense of humor. I like that a lot."

Marty smiled and blushed. She was enjoying this dinner more than anything she had done in a long, long time. She was relaxed and at ease with Will, able to tease and act silly in a way she hadn't done in years.

"So tell me what this latest project is. Maybe if I can just explain it I can keep from screwing it up the next time I show the house."

"I really am sorry for that. I was in the middle of laying out where the doors will go, and I realized I was dying of thirst. I ran down to the 7-11 for a soda, and you must have showed up just after I left. I was only gone about fifteen minutes, but by the time I got back you were in the car and gunning the engine."

"I was not gunning the engine." Marty tried a tone of mock indignation.

"Oh yes you were. I thought you were going to leave tire

tracks all the way down the street." Will's teasing tone softened. "And I felt responsible for whatever had happened. I hope you'll forgive me."

"Forgive you? Well, let me think about it." Marty pretended to ponder, wrinkling her brow and pursing her lips. "Hmmmmm. I guess . . ." she smoothed out her brow and turned up the corners of her mouth. "I guess I have to forgive anyone who makes dinner so enjoyable."

Will beamed as though he'd just won the lottery. "That was my goal, dear lady. I wanted to make it impossible for you not to forgive me, so that you would have to have dinner with me again."

"Well, let's just say that you're forgiven." Marty didn't want to examine what he said too closely, unsure if she was ready to accept a second date before the first was even over. "But you still haven't told me what this latest project is."

Will described to her his plans for enlarging the master bathroom, and opening up the bedroom by putting in sliding glass doors. It was just the way she had put it on her list, thanks to Ralph's suggestion. From what he told her, she could see the newly-remodeled room as a pleasant retreat at the end of a busy day, or a quiet spot in which to greet the morning.

Marty excused herself and went to the ladies' room. In the mirror over the sink, she could see the sparkle in her eyes and the color in her cheeks. She knew it wasn't just from the wine. She was having fun, a great deal of fun, with Will. Perhaps more fun than she should allow herself, but what harm could it be? It was just one date.

When she returned to the table, she found her chair had shifted slightly, as had Will's, so that they were sitting much closer together, facing the quiet dining room. At her place rested a small crystal dish. As she approached the table,

Will rose, and pulled out her chair for her.

"I hope French vanilla is an acceptable flavor," he said. "I was sure you'd refuse dessert if I asked, so I ordered for both of us while you were gone." Sure enough, the dish contained a scoop of French vanilla ice cream, and a crisp sugar wafer.

"How right you are, sir," she said archly. "I certainly would have refused." Then in a more normal tone she added, "But French vanilla is perfectly acceptable. Even if I am too full to truly appreciate it, I can't resist at least a taste."

She eventually finished the entire scoop, and nibbled at the cookie as they continued to talk. Marty was content to sit and listen to Will. But without realizing how skillfully he extracted the information, she told him a great deal about herself. And she knew she had told him even more by the things she didn't say.

The restaurant was nearly empty, the waiters carefully laying the empty tables for the next day's lunch. Marty suddenly noticed that even the noise in the bar had quieted considerably. She glanced at her watch, then looked again in horror. "My gosh, Will, it's nearly eleven. I have to work tomorrow morning." She looked up at him, flustered at how she had blurted out the time. Like a teenager worrying about being put on restriction for breaking curfew.

"Of course. I didn't realize it was getting so late." He rose and pulled out her chair for her. From nowhere the maitre d' appeared with her coat. The added service made her realize that Will must be well-known to the staff here. All evening there had been subtle clues, like the arrival of dessert—and the check—while she was in the ladies' room.

Clearly, this was a man accustomed to dining in the best restaurants in town, and to being treated as an honored guest in them. As she slipped her purse over her arm, she caught a movement from the corner of her eye, and realized that Will had tipped the maitre d' for his special service. No wonder they paid attention to him here.

They walked to the car in silence, Will's hand lightly cradling her elbow. She could feel the faint pressure of his fingertips against her arm, and the warmth of his touch radiated through her. The occasional brush of his arm against her side sent shivers through her. Will was so calm, so cool. She had no idea what he was thinking or feeling, and it unnerved her.

What if she had said or done something really stupid, and didn't even know it? Will was obviously a gentleman, and he would be charming and gallant right to the end of the evening. And then she would never see him again. The thought bothered her more than it should. After all, this was only one date. Besides, he *had* said that he wanted to take her out again.

He opened the car door for her, and closed it behind her after she settled in. In the brief moment of illumination from the dome light she watched his face, but she couldn't read anything in the calm, relaxed expression.

"You will have dinner with me again, won't you?" he asked as they pulled out of the parking lot. "I enjoy your company."

Marty's heart leapt in her chest, and she could feel her pulse racing. She smiled to herself. One date, and already he had her heart racing in a way Charlie never had. She refused to think about it. She was determined to take Beth's advice and just relax. This felt very good, and she certainly wanted to do it again.

"I'd love to. But I don't know if the restaurant appreciated us taking up their table for the entire evening."

"That's what they're there for, and it wasn't like we were keeping someone else from a table. That's one of the advantages of weeknights. The downside is having to let you go home this early."

The silence stretched between them. Marty imagined what it would be like to invite Will to follow her home "for a nightcap." The flutters in her stomach told her she wanted to, but they also warned her of what might happen. No, not what might happen, but what *would* happen.

Will hadn't made a single suggestive move all night, but she could feel all her senses humming. She was extremely aware of his closeness, the faint, spicy scent of his cologne lingering in the closed car, the casual masculine ease with which he drove through the quiet streets. No, this man was too tempting. She would go home alone—alone and safe. Anything more would be playing with fire, and she knew that playing with fire only got you burned.

When they reached the parking lot, Will pulled in next to her bright yellow Volkswagen Bug. Marty reached for the door handle before he could shut off the engine, intending to hop out and get in her car, but his hand on her arm stopped her.

She waited while he switched off the engine, expecting him to come around and open the door for her. Instead, he slid his arm across the back of the seat, and placed his right hand gently on her right shoulder. Her breath stopped for a fraction of a second, and she hung suspended in time, waiting, wanting but not wanting, wondering what he would do next. Would he ruin it all by coming on too strong? Would he tempt her to do what she wanted, but would regret later?

"Please, Marty, don't run away quite so fast." The hand on her shoulder turned, and his thumb ran ever-so lightly along the curve of her neck, in the same way it had run along the stem of the wineglass.

He didn't move any closer, didn't try to touch her any more than the feathery tickle along her neck, running from her earlobe to her open coat collar. His knuckle rested against the side of her throat, and she could feel her pulse pounding against the subtle pressure. Surely he could tell what effect he was having on her, yet he made no move to press the matter.

In the darkened car, she turned half-facing him. The motion pulled his hand from her neck, and she felt it settle softly between her shoulder blades. "I'm sorry, Will. But it is late, and I do need to get home." Her voice sounded small and faintly apologetic, as though she couldn't get quite enough air into her lungs to speak.

"I know." His hand pressed against her back with a gentle insistence. "I just hate to see the evening end. I've had a wonderful time tonight, and I don't want to let you go, even though I know I have to."

The pressure increased ever so slightly, and he leaned toward her. Carefully, stretching to reach her without moving any closer, he touched his lips to hers. His kiss was firm, yet gentle, holding her mouth in its soft embrace.

She could taste a faint trace of chocolate from the mud pie he'd had for dessert, and smell his heady, masculine fragrance—a combination of his cologne and his personal scent. As his lips lingered on hers, she drank in his scent, and felt her insides turn to jelly. She pulled her mouth from his, and leaned her tingling forehead against his shoulder, afraid she wouldn't be able to sit up by herself.

Will pulled her closer, moving slightly from under the steering wheel, until their bodies touched, and he could put both arms around her. His hands laid still against her back, fingers splayed across her shoulder blades. Even through her coat, the sensation of his touch made her shiver. He took one hand from her back, and softly cupped her chin, tilting her face up to look at her in the faint glow from the street lights.

"You're an amazing woman, Ms. Francis," he said. His mouth lowered to briefly taste hers once again. "And a beautiful one." The next kiss was longer, more aggressive. Marty responded, meeting his hunger with her own. She could feel the longing within her grow, a heat and hunger she had denied for so long. She pressed against him, savoring the feel of his strong, hard chest.

His hands held the back of her head, his fingers tangled in her curls. His tongue played against her lips, seeking hers. Her lips parted, and she accepted him. She ran her hands over his face, rubbing her knuckles over the faint stubble of his cheek, trailing a fingertip along his ear, finally burying her fingers in the soft hair at the nape of his neck. She moaned deep in her throat, and arched her body tightly against Will.

She was growing too warm in her coat. She should take it off, it was too hot, and it was in the way. If she could just untie the belt.

With a gasp, she wrenched herself from Will's embrace. Her face was flaming, whether from passion or shame she couldn't be sure. Not that it mattered. She had to stop this now.

"Sorry," she gasped, gulping deep breaths of the over-heated air. "I got a little carried away." He reached for her, but she backed away, pushing his hands back. "No, please. Let me catch my breath, then I have to go."

In the dark, she couldn't be sure of Will's expression, but she could hear the combination of patience and disappointment in his voice. "I should be apologizing to you. I didn't mean to come on so strong."

He waited a minute, while they both struggled to control their breathing, and Marty's heart slowed to a more normal rate. "But Marty, I do hope you'll give me another chance. I wouldn't want it to end like this."

Marty nodded. She didn't trust her voice quite yet. She swallowed hard, and raised shaking hands to straighten the combs which had come loose from her hair. That done, she adjusted the collar of her coat, and picked up her purse. Finally she felt secure enough to speak. "I have to go."

It was Will's turn to nod. He got out and opened her door for her, offering her his hand to help her from the car. She gingerly took his hand, maintaining a distance between them as she stepped to her car.

When she had the door opened, Will caught her wrist, and pulled her toward him. He kissed her lightly on the cheek, carefully avoiding any other contact. He laughed, a little shakily. "Can I call you tomorrow?"

Marty nodded. "Um-hmm. I . . . I'd like that. Good night now." Before she could change her mind, she ducked into the car and started the engine. She let it idle for a couple minutes to defrost the windshield, then backed out of her parking space and headed home. In the rearview mirror, she could see Will watching her until she turned the corner and he disappeared from sight.

Will watched the brake lights on the Beetle flash as Marty reached the corner. She paused at the intersection, and then she was gone, around the corner and out of sight.

What an idiot he had been! Get his arms around a pretty girl, and he nearly smothered her. No wonder she ran like a scared rabbit.

Scowling at his own screw-up, Will started the car and pulled out of the parking lot. He knew he was too keyed-up to sleep, too annoyed at himself to relax.

There was one thing that he did on nights like this to calm down. He focused on work. He patted his jacket pocket, making sure his little notebook was there, and turned toward the closest job site. A quick tour of his current projects would make him feel better.

However, as he drove, his thoughts kept drifting back to Marty. She was attractive, certainly, with her red hair and soft brown eyes. She was small, but still round in all the right places, and she clearly kept herself in good shape.

But those were just the obvious things. There were other, more important things, that attracted him to her. The quick intelligence when she talked. Her easy laughter, and her sense of humor.

She refused to take herself too seriously, but she was serious about her work, and good at what she did. She had a reputation for honesty, something very important to Will.

Face it. She was the whole package, and he had very nearly blown it. But she had said he could call tomorrow, and he planned to make up for tonight's fiasco. Just as quickly as he could.

Driving past the third job site, he realized he hadn't really seen any of the three. He assured himself he would have noticed anything out of the ordinary, gave up, and turned toward home. This wasn't getting him any closer to sleeping, and it was after midnight.

He pulled into the driveway of his building, and slid his keycard into the garage lock. The light blinked, and the door to the underground parking garage slid open. His space was halfway between the door and the elevator, and the door had closed and re-locked itself before he shut off the engine.

When he unlocked the door to his condo, the red light on the answering machine was shining steadily. No messages. He got most of his calls at the office, and he preferred it that way. Here, in the small apartment he called home, he could be alone and there were few people he knew well enough to give them the private number.

Tonight, though, he felt an odd disappointment at the quiet. Had he been nursing some illusion that Marty would call? Even if she had wanted to, she didn't have the number. Not that he thought she would want to.

Will tried to shake off the unaccustomed fit of melancholy. It was the talk of Karen, he was sure. He seldom mentioned her, and most of his acquaintances didn't know about his wife, or that he had ever been married.

He had brought it up, after all, by asking Marty if she was married. He could have, *should* have, expected her question in return. And he should have been prepared to answer it. He had thought he was fine, glossing over his loss, but the stricken look on Marty's face had forced him to speak more freely than he had meant to.

It wasn't that he had forgotten about Karen, but more that he didn't remember her constantly, as he had at first. Then, she had occupied every waking moment, and lived in his dreams. Now, he thought about her only in unguarded moments.

He hung his jacket in the closet, and put his pants on the valet chair, emptying the pockets into the tray on his dresser. He dropped his shirt into the bag for the cleaners, and wrapped himself in a lightweight terrycloth robe cinching the belt around his waist.

He left a lamp on in the bedroom. In the dim light that

spilled down the hallway to the living room, he crossed to the drapes and pulled them open.

The city lay spread out below him, stretching to the dark shapes of the low foothills that surrounded it. Streetlamps outlined the thoroughfares, straight lines that wavered and swirled as they reached the hills.

Will grabbed a soda from the refrigerator, the bright interior light temporarily leaving him blinded. With a skill born of familiarity, he walked between the few pieces of furniture and settled into his battered recliner.

The chair was comfortable, molding itself to him the way an old pair of shoes molded themselves to his feet. He finally began to unwind, letting go of the tension and turmoil the evening had aroused.

Watching the lights, Will considered calling Marty. Just to make sure she had made it home safely. Just to be sure she was safe.

Though the temptation of hearing her voice was strong, reason prevailed. It was the middle of the night. She would be asleep, and she wouldn't welcome a call that woke her up. Especially not a call from the man she had run away from an hour earlier.

He imagined what she might think if he did call at this hour. At best, he would come off as a pathetic loser, or an insensitive jerk. Worse, he might look like some kind of stalker. Better to wait until tomorrow.

With a tired sigh, Will closed the drapes and headed for the shower. In a few minutes, he would be in bed, and he would not think about Marty Francis until, at least, the morning.

Maybe.

Chapter 15

Marty's machine was blinking four messages when she walked in the front door. She wanted to ignore them, to curl up in her sofa cushions and relive every minute of her evening with Will.

She compromised. Slowly and carefully she undressed, removed her makeup, and showered. Through it all, she played back the evening in her mind. The way Will laughed. The stories he told her. The way he listened, really listened, to what she had to say.

She marveled again and again at how much they agreed on, from no beets in their salads, to action-adventure movies. But mostly she remembered the feel of his hands on her back, his arms crushing her against him, his lips on hers. Each time she thought of those minutes locked in his embrace, she could feel the heat rise in her body, the lovely fluttery feeling in her stomach.

She remembered his voice saying, "And a beautiful one," replaying the words again and again. She heard the passion as he had murmured her name while they clung to one another. She caught the faint memory of his scent as she put her coat on its hook, and buried her face against it, allowing herself the luxury of once again savoring that unique scent.

Eventually her clothes were put away, her shower was done, her face was scrubbed clean, and she forced herself to put her memories away for a while. She carefully packed them into the place in her memory reserved for special moments, ones she could retrieve later and examine slowly, warming herself with their beauty.

For now, it was nearly one o'clock in the morning, she had to get up and go to work in a few hours, and she had better check the answering machine, in case there was something important.

The first message was from Beth, wishing her good luck with her date. She had called about seven, not realizing that Marty was meeting Will at the office. Then there was a message from the office, changing an appointment for the next day from nine a.m. to one p.m. Marty breathed a little sigh of relief. That meant she could sleep in a little later. The last two messages were also from Beth, each a little more insistent than the last. One had been about nine-thirty, and Beth's voice teased her from the tinny speaker.

"You must be having a good time, since you aren't home yet. I certainly hope you're following Auntie Beth's advice and enjoying yourself. I'll be up 'til about eleven, call me if you're home by then. Bye."

The next call had the same bantering tone, but underneath there was an element of concern. "It's past eleven. Are you staying out past your curfew? I was just checking in with you before I went to bed, but you call me if you need me, you hear? Otherwise, I'll expect you to call first thing tomorrow and tell me *all* about it. Take care."

Marty sighed. She would have to tell Beth about it, but she squirmed a little at the thought of describing the adolescent groping that had ended the evening. Maybe she could just leave that part out when she called Beth. No, Beth always knew when Marty wasn't telling her everything. She had been that way when Beth met Charlie, and later, when the marriage was going sour. She wouldn't be able to get away without giving Beth all the juicy details.

Marty puttered around the house another few minutes, taking care of the little homey chores that made up her nightly routine. Water the plants, reset the answering machine, change the alarm to let her sleep an hour later, and get the coffee pot ready for morning.

All the while, her thoughts kept wandering to Will. Try as she might to concentrate on what she was doing, his face kept coming unbidden into her thoughts. His smile, the set of his jaw, the way his hair fell over his ears. She set the timer on the coffee pot, and wondered what he was doing right this minute.

She had to get past this moony teenage behavior. You'd think she'd never had a date in her life. Although, when she thought about it, this was the first real date she had had in nearly six years.

Her first date since Charlie. Somehow, the times they went out while they were married didn't feel like dates. She knew there were married couples who went out on dates with each other on a regular basis.

Fred, who'd covered for her tonight, talked about his dates with his wife. And she knew Dotty and her husband had dates together, when Dotty's mother kept the baby overnight.

But what she and Charlie had never felt like dates. They felt like conveniences. Having dinner out because they were both too tired or too busy to cook. Going to the mall because they could each do their individual errands and shopping.

She'd been amazed when Fred told her he and his wife

sometimes went out for a burger and then played pinball at the arcade in the mall, sometimes for hours.

Marty couldn't imagine Charlie ever playing pinball; there was something too uncontrolled about the game. But she could see Will standing over a game table, lights flashing on his face, as he laughed and nudged and grimaced. She would have to ask him if he played.

She had forgotten about pinball when Will asked her about her luxuries tonight. A pinball date with Will sounded like fun.

A lot of things with Will sounded like fun.

Okay, so she was a little out of practice at this dating thing. But that didn't mean she should go around making more of things than they were. It was just one date, just a couple of kisses. After all, Will was a bit older, and more sophisticated. Maybe he had just expected more on a first date.

The rules may have changed since the days of casual sex, but some of that was new since she had been dating. And casual sex had never been a part of her world, anyway.

More confused than ever, Marty turned out the lights and headed for bed. Maybe in the morning it would make more sense. For that matter, maybe she ought to talk to Beth. Beth had jumped back into the swim of dating almost immediately after the hasty departure of her deadbeat husband. Beth would know what the rules were.

Having decided to ask Beth's advice, Marty settled into her bed, and shut off the lamp on her nightstand. But laying alone in the dark and quiet, the feel of Will's lips and the smell of his body lingered, and followed her into her dreams.

Chapter 16

The ringing of the telephone woke Marty from a dream of Will, of his hands and his lips, of his soft gray eyes, his hearty laughter and quiet conversation. Disoriented, she swatted at the alarm clock, trying to silence the insistent ringing. When her palm thumping the snooze button failed to bring the desired result, she roused herself further and heard the answering machine pick up.

Good, the answering machine is doing its job. She rolled over, determined to go back to sleep until the alarm really did wake her. But she couldn't break the habit of listening, and she could hear the beep as the machine began recording.

"Marty?" Beth's voice was clearly worried. "Marty, are you home yet? I called the office, but they said you weren't in yet, and I'm starting to get worried about where you are. You went on that stupid date, and I kept telling you . . ."

Marty stumbled from the bedroom into the office and picked up the receiver.

"For heaven's sake, Beth, can't a person sleep in without you going into a panic?"

"Marty?" Beth's voice sounded weak with relief. "I was really beginning to worry about you, when you weren't home by late last night, and I didn't hear from you this morning." She paused to take a deep breath, then demanded, "Where were you, anyway?"

"Beth, you're starting to sound like my mother. There's a reason I live five hundred miles from her, y'know."

"So? You're a little rusty at this dating stuff, somebody has to look after you."

Marty laughed. Here was Beth, who had urged her to go out and have fun, worrying like a mother hen.

"You think this is funny? There are a lot of weird people out there. Believe me, I know. I think I've probably dated most of them. And you just aren't ready to deal with 'em."

"Hold on, Beth. Just take it easy. Can I call you back in five minutes? I just woke up. I need a cup of coffee and a few minutes to pull myself together, then we can talk."

"I have a better idea. I just got back from the Chamber of Commerce breakfast, and I don't have anything on the schedule for the next couple hours. If you're free, I'll just stop over there instead of going to the office. And," she continued sternly, "I expect a full report on where you went and what you did last night. I really was worried, you know."

"I give up." Marty chuckled. "Come on over. In the time it will take you to get here I can have the coffee made and my hair combed, but you'll probably have to put up with my bathrobe."

"I don't care if you're wearing a Halloween costume. I'll be there in ten minutes."

True to her word, Beth was at the door in ten minutes. Marty was still in her bathrobe, but she had managed to get coffee made, and put some canned refrigerator biscuits in the toaster oven. She was setting butter and strawberry jam on the trestle table when the doorbell rang. She called to Beth to come in, and went back to the kitchen for the coffee pot and cups. The oven timer beeped, and she took the biscuits out. Balancing a plate of biscuits on top of the coffee, she walked back to the dining room, where Beth had seated herself on one of the benches alongside the table.

"Well? Was it awful?" Beth jumped up and took the biscuits, which were threatening to slide off the coffee pot and tumble to the floor. She set them on the table, and took a cup from Marty, who poured coffee for both of them.

"No, it wasn't awful." Marty sat on the opposite bench, and busied herself buttering a biscuit, and spooning jam into the middle of it. She held the plate out to Beth, trying to maintain an innocent look. "Would you like a biscuit?"

"Marty!" Beth was ready to explode from frustration. Her mouth twitched, and laughter bubbled up from inside her. "You are being a brat, and you know it. You promised to tell me all about last night, and now you sit here offering me biscuits, when you know I just had breakfast."

"Oh, did you have breakfast already?" Marty's feigned innocence was straining, and she struggled to keep a straight face. "Why, that's right, I believe you did. You had that Chamber of Commerce thing this morning, didn't you? How was it, did you enjoy your breakfast?"

Beth rolled her eyes, and the two friends dissolved in giggles. Beth grabbed a biscuit from the plate, and threatened to hurl it across the table, and Marty finally waved her napkin in surrender.

"About time," Beth said, lowering the ammunition. "You have been refusing to tell me what happened for practically hours now, and I want to know." Her voice turned serious, as she watched Marty relax. "I really was worried about you, but it's clear *something* interesting went on. Now you be a good girl, and tell me all about it while I have another cup of coffee."

Marty sobered, carefully arranging her biscuit on her plate. She kept her eyes downcast as she toyed with the food in front of her. "It was wonderful," she said softly. "Will is, I don't quite know what he is. He's smart, and funny, and he looks good, and we talked for hours." She looked up, meeting Beth's eyes. "That's all we did, really, was talk. We went to dinner, and we stayed there until they practically had to throw us out. All the waiters seem to know him, and the service he gets is incredible." She paused for a sip of coffee.

"Go on . . ."

"I don't know what else to tell you, exactly. We found out we have a lot in common, and we laughed a lot, and then he took me back to pick up my car."

"You took your own car?"

"No. I just had him pick me up at the office. I was a little scared to have him pick me up here. You keep telling me to be careful, there are a lot of weirdoes out there. That way, he didn't know where I live." She grinned at Beth. "See? I have been listening to your warnings."

"So he took me back to the office to pick up my car, and then I came home." Marty could feel the telltale blush creeping up her cheeks as she remembered what had happened in between, and she quickly reached for the coffee pot, hoping Beth wouldn't see the color giving her away.

But of course she did.

"And that was it? That's all that happened? I don't think so, dearie, not from the way you're blushing just talking about it. There was a little more to it than that. You're holding out on me." Beth's tone was bantering, but Marty heard a tone of concern beneath the light words. Beth had encouraged her to relax and have a good time, but Marty could tell Beth was worried whether she had given the right advice.

"Well, he did kiss me goodnight."

"I've never known you to blush that way over a simple kiss goodnight."

"You've never seen me after a first date, either. You have to remember, Beth, this is the first guy I've been out with since I started dating Charlie. That's over six years, and I'm kinda out of practice. I don't even know what the rules are any more. In fact, I had planned to call you when I got up," she glanced significantly at her watch, "which should have been in about fifteen minutes, to ask you about this whole dating thing."

"What about it?"

Marty stirred her coffee, though she had added neither sugar nor cream. She took a deep breath, and plunged ahead. "He kissed me, all right. In fact, he kissed me a lot, and I really liked it. But it's been so long I don't know quite how to act, and I don't know what's expected, or acceptable, or anything.

"I remember when we were in high school, and everybody was 'doing it' with their steadies. And for a while it seemed like it was just assumed that if a guy asked you out more than once, you'd end up in bed somewhere. But now there's AIDS, and I keep hearing about the 'new chastity,' and I'm so confused by the whole thing."

Beth nodded sympathetically. "I understand your problem. It's the same one I have."

"You? You act like you've got all the answers, and you date all the time. You must know what to do."

"The only answer I have is to do what feels right for you, and for who you're with. And you have to be safe about it. I gather from what you said that you came home alone."

"Yes, not that I wanted to, but it scared me. He was so different from the other men, boys really, that I dated. And he's so very different from Charlie . . .

"Beth, I have a really weird question, but it's driving me nuts. Did you ever meet anybody that *smelled* right? I don't mean like he wears the right cologne, or he doesn't smoke. I mean he just has a smell all his own, and it's made up of little parts of everything about him—his clothes, his soap, his aftershave—and it all adds up to something special." Marty sputtered to a stop, feeling incredibly foolish for blurting out such a stupid question.

"He smells right?" Marty was listening for derision or disbelief in Beth's voice, but her question held a note of something closer to envy.

Startled, Marty nodded. "I know that sounds weird, but it's true. I mean, there was lots to like about him, but I kept noticing how he smelled. In a good way, I mean. You know, you can notice how a person smells and it isn't good, but it wasn't like that."

"I've never actually met anyone that I thought smelled exactly right," Beth said, "but I have heard about it from other people. And it's always from people that are in good, solid relationships. Not that it's anything to base your whole life on, but it sure sounds like a good sign to me."

Marty blushed again, and sighed softly.

"You really liked him, didn't you?" Beth asked, a note of concern in her voice.

"You know, I really did. Just everything about him was so great. You know what he did?" Marty asked.

Beth shook her head, waiting for Marty to continue.

"I told him I like ice cream, so when I went to the ladies' room he had the waiter bring me ice cream for dessert. He said he knew I would turn down dessert if he asked, so he didn't ask, he just ordered it for me." Marty smiled at the memory.

"I know, I know," she continued, reaching for another biscuit. "He sounds like some kind of control freak, not giving me the chance to make up my own mind. But he wasn't; he was just sweet and thoughtful. It was like his way of letting me know he'd really been listening."

Visibly more relaxed, Marty chattered on, telling Beth detail after detail about her date, and about Will.

She admitted that he had asked to see her again, and that she hadn't said no.

Beth poured herself another cup of coffee, and reached for a biscuit. "You didn't say no, but did you say yes? That's the important question."

"I did at first, but that was before we, well, you know." Marty blushed again, remembering the feel of Will's arms around her and his lips on hers. "But he did ask if he could call me today, and I said yes to that."

"You had better say yes to him. Judging from what I can see, this is the best thing to happen to you in a long time. Enjoy it."

Chapter 17

Marty arrived at the office in high spirits. She'd had a good visit with Beth, and she still carried the afterglow of the previous evening. She was even too happy to be bothered by the teasing she received when Lorraine noticed her vanity case had been left in the bathroom overnight.

Lorraine stopped her next to the coffee pot, cup in hand.

"You didn't even come back for your clothes?" she asked.

"It was late when I picked up the car, and I didn't figure there was anything I couldn't live without." Marty didn't want to admit that the steamy scene in the parking lot had taken all other thoughts from her head, and that she had simply forgotten her work clothes were still in the office.

"Must have been good, to keep you out after dark. Who was he?" Lorraine was about as subtle as a brick. Marty just laughed.

"Just this guy I met while I was showing a house. Nothing to get excited about." Marty turned to head back to her desk.

"Doesn't look that way from here," Lorraine said to her retreating back. "I haven't seen you look like this in a long time."

Marty stopped and turned around, her curiosity getting

the better of her. "Like what?"

"Oh, I don't know." Lorraine waved her hand airily. "Smiling like you know a secret the rest of us don't. The sparkle in your eyes, the bounce in your step. Especially first thing in the morning."

"It's not first thing in the morning, it's eleven o'clock." Marty affected nonchalance, sipping her coffee and pretending to study a brochure for a seminar on "Time Management for Women" that was posted on the bulletin board.

"And you just got in. 'Methinks the lady doth protest too much,' " she said, and grinned at Marty. "I think it must have been a pretty good evening. And I can't wait to see who's responsible for all this."

"Oh, good grief." Marty turned to face Lorraine. "At least you're not as bad as Beth. *She* was at my door at eight-thirty this morning, demanding to know all the details."

Lorraine laughed, her coffee sloshing dangerously in her mug. "Maybe that's what I should have done. Then at least I'd know who he was." She stopped suddenly, realizing that she had nearly slopped coffee on her ivory silk blouse.

"See what happens when you get nosy?" Marty made a silly face at Lorraine, stopping just short of sticking her tongue out, and went back to her desk.

Why, she wondered, did everyone seem to think they could give her this third-degree about a simple date? Probably, she told herself, because they knew she hadn't had a real date in years, and Marty on a real, honest-to-goodness date was a whole new phenomenon. She shrugged. They had better get used to it, because she had discovered she liked dating. Or at least, she discovered she liked dating Will.

She settled at her desk, and dug into the pile of mail and messages that had accumulated during the morning. She would have to concentrate and work through lunch to make up for the time she had missed in the morning. She began sorting the paper into stacks: calls to return, letters to answer, listings to check. She picked up the list of messages, and started working her way through them.

Early in the afternoon, her phone rang. She picked it up, still focused on the offer/counter-offer she was putting together for a client, and answered automatically, "Good afternoon, Marty Francis. Can I help you?"

"I sure hope so." The already-familiar sound of Will's voice startled her. She dropped the paper she had been studying, and felt a decidedly unprofessional warmth creep into her voice as she answered him.

"Hi. How are you?"

They chatted amiably for a couple minutes. All the while, Marty's mind raced. He had called. But why? He didn't seem to have anything particular to talk about. Not that it mattered to her. It was enough that he called.

She could see that Lorraine had noticed the change in her, and was eyeing her with frank curiosity across the office. Marty turned her chair, putting her back to Lorraine's questioning glances.

"I wanted to thank you for last night," Will was saying. "I had a wonderful time, and I was hoping you hadn't changed your mind about seeing me again."

"Why would I do that?" Marty's heart was pounding in her throat. Maybe he was trying to brush her off. Maybe he thought the evening had ended badly, and he was trying to smooth things over.

There was a pause at the other end of the line, and then Will cleared his throat. "Because, frankly, I got the feeling I had come on a bit too strong. I was afraid I had scared you away for good."

Marty's answering laugh was shaky with relief. He was worried how *she* felt. So she hadn't botched it after all. "Oh no, Will. I'm just out of practice."

"Dating, I mean," she added hastily. "It's been a long time, and I have a hunch some things have changed in the last few years."

"Perhaps, but what hasn't changed is enjoying the company of a lovely young woman. Which is why I called you. I'd like you to have dinner with me again. Tonight, if you're free."

The invitation was so sudden and unexpected that Marty didn't have time to think it over. "I'd love to," she blurted out.

"Great! I've got some work to do at the house this afternoon, but I should be through early. What time is good for you?"

"Is six okay? I am going to have to make it an early evening," Marty said, frantically digging in her battered old briefcase to check her appointment book. "I have a couple of early appointments tomorrow."

"Six is fine. Where shall I pick you up?"

Decision time, Marty told herself. Did she want Will to pick her up at home, or did she want the safety net of having her own car at the office? And did she need to go home to change? She quickly assessed her outfit—dark green wool pants, a plaid jacket, and cream-colored blouse in a simple style—and decided she wanted to change for dinner. So home it would be. "Would you mind picking me up at home? I'll need to change clothes after work."

Will agreed without hesitation. Marty hoped she hadn't implied anything by the invitation, as she gave him the address and directions on how to find it. She hung up, already trying to second-guess his invitation and her response. She kept telling herself to relax and enjoy whatever came along, but little shivers of anticipation, or perhaps of memory, kept running down her spine at unexpected moments.

"So?" Lorraine had approached while Marty was still sorting out her tangled emotions. She stood over the desk with a question in her eyes, and her hands on her hips. "Was that Prince Charming? No, never mind. You don't need to answer that, it's written all over your face. Whoever he is, he must be something, because you are positively glowing."

Marty felt the color rising in her cheeks. "Lorraine! For heaven's sake, cut it out."

Lorraine laughed good-naturedly and patted Marty on the shoulder. "Don't get excited. It just does my heart good to see you coming out of that shell you've been hiding in for the last three years. You got divorced, but you didn't die, you know, and it's about time you realized that. Now get out there and enjoy yourself."

"You know, you're the second person this week to tell me that," Marty said, remembering her breakfast with Beth. "This seems to be the universal plan you all have for me." She sighed theatrically, "So I suppose I shall simply *have* to have fun. You would all be so disappointed if I didn't." She looked up at Lorraine, her eyes twinkling.

Lorraine fell into the playful spirit, replying, "See that you do. I do so hate to be disappointed. Especially because someone failed to follow my marvelous advice."

Marty wasn't inclined to offer any more details, and Lorraine eventually wandered back to her desk. But she still kept stealing occasional glances at Marty, who resolutely focused on her work, while checking the clock every fifteen minutes.

On the dot of five-fifteen, Marty closed up her briefcase,

put away her papers, and zipped out the door before anyone could delay her exit. She drove home as quickly as she dared, and found herself with barely half an hour to prepare herself for her date with Will. She vowed to keep to her plan of an early night, though. No sense in tempting fate by spending endless hours with a man who made her feel weak in the knees, and warm everywhere else.

The bathroom, Will decided, was a *monster*. He had a few other words for it, too. None of them was nearly as polite.

Marty had said kitchens and bathrooms sold a house. He had seen a design for a whirlpool tub set in a bay window, with a fenced flower garden just outside, and he knew the garden tub would make the bathroom a high point. What he hadn't counted on was the amount of work involved in removing the tub, wall, and tiny bathroom window, and replacing them with a bay window, whirlpool tub, and tile.

Before he could tackle any of the demolition or construction, he had to order the window. He pulled the end of the tape measure across the back wall once again. He had measured the blasted wall three times now, but each time he had forgotten the measurement in the time it took to walk to the counter and write it down.

Will never had this kind of problem, but he knew what the trouble was. Each time he took the measurement, he could envision the garden window and whirlpool tub he had planned for the space. And each time, he would imagine a certain beautiful young woman enjoying the luxurious bath.

It was ridiculous. He hadn't been this distracted by a girl since he was sixteen, and completely obsessed with one of the junior varsity cheerleaders. But he wasn't sixteen any more, not by a long shot, and Marty wasn't a girl. She was a woman, and he had ample evidence of that in the few minutes they had been close.

Clearing the enticing pictures from his imagination, he started over. This time, as he noted the width of the window space, he focused on the steps of the installation, refusing to think about the finished project until he had the measurements safely recorded in his notebook.

With his notes made and double-checked, he grabbed his cell phone and made a quick call to his window supplier. The sales rep suggested a custom window, but the delivery would take three or four weeks.

Waiting was not one of Will's strengths when he was immersed in a project. There was a standard-size bay window in a size that would fit the wall, and he immediately ordered it, instead. That window he could have in two days.

Will looked around, assessing the rest of the work. The whirlpool tub was scheduled for delivery this morning, along with a new sink and toilet. All he had to do was get the old ones out.

Taking out the old fixtures, though, was much easier said than done. Will shut off the water, disconnected the sink, and wrestled it out of the vanity. The new base cabinet was waiting, and he manhandled it into position. He finally had to admit that he would need help mounting and leveling.

He glanced at his watch. The delivery had been promised for morning, and it was already after two. No wonder he was hungry. If he left to get lunch, the delivery truck was sure to arrive. Or maybe a certain red-headed real estate agent would stop by. Either way, he wasn't taking any chances. He would stay put.

In the kitchen, he peered in the refrigerator. There was an apple left from earlier in the week. He bit into it as he went back down the hall.

The apple didn't hold him for long, and soon his stomach was grumbling. He ignored its protests, promising himself a hearty dinner.

Dinner. Marty. He took another quick look at his watch. Nearly three. He had promised to pick her up at six. There was at least an hour's paperwork waiting at the office; checks to sign for the week's materials, and a payroll to approve.

That truck had better get here soon.

By the time the bathroom fixtures arrived, Will had disconnected the toilet, and started on the tub. As the driver presented him the bill of lading for signature, Will checked the time again. Four-fifteen.

He quickly scrawled his name across the bottom of the receipt and handed it back to the driver. With the help of a power lift, they got the boxes down the hall and into the bedroom before the driver left.

Will stood alone in the bedroom, which was now crowded with heavy boxes. There was a lot more to do in the bathroom, but if he didn't leave soon, he would be late to pick up Marty.

He was used to simple, straightforward priorities. Things were done in order, according to a carefully-laid-out timetable. But Marty had thrown all of that out the window for him. Now, instead of following his schedule, he quit what he was doing and headed home.

He stopped at the office, flipped through the paperwork, and signed off on the payroll. A subcontractor was asking for another day on the auto dealer's service building, which would delay the plumber. He initialed the change, with a note to Rita, his secretary, to reschedule the plumbing sub. The rest, including next week's orders, could be done later.

Just like the Bakers' bathroom.

Will hated putting things off. There wasn't enough time for everything, but that had never stopped him. Although they never said it to his face, he knew his college buddies had tagged him with "Where there's a Will, there's a way." That had never changed.

He stopped with his hand on the doorknob, realizing an opportunity had just presented itself. Turning back to the desk, he pulled the sticky note from the work order, and changed Rita's instructions. He would have the plumber meet him at the Agate house instead. No sense in letting a chance like this go to waste.

With his immediate problems taken care of, Will locked up the office and headed home. He just had time to shower before dinner. Everything else could wait.

Right now, his top priority had red hair, and a great sense of humor.

Marty dashed through the shower, piled her hair up and held it in place with a couple combs, then spent ten precious minutes carefully applying fresh makeup. Wearing a slip and a pair of pantyhose, she pawed through her closet, looking for just the right thing to wear. She finally gave up, tossed the slip on the bed, and settled on a pair of fawn colored wool slacks, a dark green silk turtleneck, and the plaid jacket she had worn to the office, with its touches of the same green as her turtleneck.

She stood in front of the full-length mirror on the bedroom door, studying the effect with a critical eye. The green was a good color with her coppery red hair and pale complexion, and the richness of the wool and silk offset the casual outfit. She slipped into a pair of plain, camel-colored two-inch pumps. With Will, she needed heels.

She would fit in almost anywhere in town with this outfit, she decided. Which was a good thing, since she didn't know exactly where Will had in mind for dinner.

When she opened the door for Will, he was wearing blue jeans, with a brown tweed sports coat over a pale yellow shirt of oxford cloth. Marty congratulated herself on selecting just the right note of casual elegance to match his. Will made a show of looking her up and down, then nodding in approval.

"I was right the first time. You are the prettiest real estate salesperson in town."

"You don't look too bad yourself," Marty replied. Taking her purse from the coat rack next to the door, she stepped outside and pulled the door closed behind her. She carefully locked the deadbolt, and checked to be sure it was firmly latched.

Catching Will's look of amusement, she blushed and laughed. "Too many years of going in and out of other people's houses," she explained. "I just got in the habit of double-checking the locks every time I leave a house."

Will nodded. "Occupational hazard, I guess," he said, and followed her down the front walk to where his car was parked at the curb.

As Will drove, he talked to her about his day, and the work he was doing on the house. "You might not want to take anyone over there for a couple more days," he warned her. "The master bathroom and bedroom project turned out to be a little more work than I had expected, and it still isn't quite finished. In fact," he glanced at her, disappointment clear on his face, "I have to hire a plumber to finish up some of the work."

"You can't expect to be able to do everything yourself, Will. And even if you did, you'd still have to have a licensed plumber come in to certify the work. Without that, you'll have a devil of a time with the city construction permits."

"I suppose. But it was like admitting defeat when I finally decided to call him. It was the first time the house has managed to beat me." He grinned, his even, white teeth flashing. "I guess I'm one of those guys that always has to win."

Marty digested this bit of information, knowing it was an important clue to Will Hart, a part of him she would be wise to remember.

She realized he had carefully avoided any discussion of where they were going for dinner, unlike their previous date when he had checked with her before they arrived at the restaurant. Tonight he not only seemed to have a destination firmly in mind, but he was being secretive about it. Marty wondered what he was up to.

She didn't have to wait long to find out. Much to Marty's surprise, in just a few minutes they pulled into the parking lot of a local restaurant, decked out like a turn-of-the-century ice cream parlor.

Will shut off the engine and turned to face her in the dusky evening light. "You said you love ice cream, so I figured this had to be the place to take you. I hope you don't think it's too corny." His voice rose, questioning, at the end of his sentence.

Her momentary shock had passed, and Marty realized how touched she was by his choice. He had actually thought about what she liked, and what might please her. "It's not at all corny, it's sweet. I love this place, and I almost never come here. I'm not even sure why. Just never think of it, I guess. Or maybe I don't trust myself with that much ice cream."

Once they were seated at their table, and had placed

their orders, Will looked at her across the table. "This was really okay?"

"It's great." Marty's voice bubbled with barely-suppressed hilarity. "There is something so relentlessly cheerful about this place, it's impossible not to have a good time. I don't know why there aren't more of them around, but this is the only one I know of."

"They were all the rage for a while, but their popularity dropped. They all closed down years ago, except for this one and one other down in San Diego. I'll have to take you there sometime."

The implication of his words hung in the air between them, a palpable presence. The future stretched in front of both of them, beckoning them on. Marty felt herself being pulled along; and letting go, going for the ride to see where it would take her, seemed like the best idea in the world.

"Maybe so," she said. Her green eyes met Will's gray ones, and sparks seemed to fly across the table. His hand reached out and took hers, starting the jolts of electricity again. He squeezed her fingers lightly, and she pressed his in return.

"It's a date, then," he said. "We'll work out the details later." They both laughed at the absurdity of it, but Marty felt a secret flare of hope growing in her chest. Maybe, just maybe, this was for real. Maybe there was something to Beth's theory that he was "the one" if he smelled right. And maybe she didn't have to worry so much about the way her stomach swooped and her head swam every time he looked at her.

Just relax and enjoy the ride.

Will watched Marty while they ate burgers, and joined in singing "Happy Birthday" to a pair of four-year-old twins, a gray-haired woman whose granddaughter announced she was "eighty-three years young," and a giggling teenaged girl who arrived surrounded by a gaggle of other giggling, self-conscious teenaged girls.

Marty kept looking at the group of girls, and Will wondered what she had been like when she was that young. Had she been as confident and self-assured as she was now? Looking at the graceful woman she had become, he found it hard to imagine her as a gangly, awkward teenager.

"Hard to believe we were ever that young, isn't it?" he asked, nodding toward the table. Another fit of giggling erupted. The birthday girl shushed the group, her face flaming, but her smile bright.

Marty looked at him, smiling. "I was just thinking the same thing." She laughed, a small, embarrassed sound. "Sometimes I think I never got past that stage."

A blush filled her face with color. She was cute when she blushed, and she looked like she wasn't much more than a kid herself.

"I like it." He had thought it, but he hadn't meant to say it out loud.

Marty grew redder, and put her hand to her face, as if to hide the growing color. He reached over and pulled her hand away.

"Don't. I like the fact that there are still women in this world who blush." He held her hand, keeping it away from her face. "Besides, it's kinda cute."

He liked the feel of her hand, the softness of her skin and the warmth of her touch. He couldn't remember the last time he had enjoyed such a simple thing with a woman.

She pulled her hand away, and the warmth left him. She took a long drink of water, and he watched the color subside from her face. Still, she refused to meet his gaze.

Will insisted that she eat ice cream with him, and dismissed her protests that ice cream two nights in a row would immediately take up permanent residence on her hips. "If it does, we'll just have to run it off on the tennis court. That is, if you'll play against a decrepit old man with a lousy serve and a weak backhand."

"I think you're sandbagging. You probably have a killer backhand, and a monster serve. Besides, the weather's lousy for tennis."

"Not if you play indoors. You said you had a membership somewhere, as I recall. There aren't that many clubs in town. We could belong to the same club, and then you'd have no excuse."

"But it's crowded in the winter . . ."

"Not if you go early in the afternoon."

"I have to work . . ."

"You have flexible hours. Besides, you work on the weekends, so you can take some time off during the week."

He enjoyed sparring with her, countering every objection with a logical answer. Or an illogical answer, if it amused her. Her eyes sparkled, telling him she was playing along with his game.

Seeing her here, relaxed, being silly, was a huge contrast with their elegant and serious dinner of the previous night. Will hoped that the awkward ending of their previous dinner had been forgotten, or at least forgiven.

Will seemed to have an answer to every objection Marty could muster, though she was having fun trying to stump him. Maybe this was another time to relax and see where it went. She capitulated, grinning at Will. "I can see that there is absolutely no sense in arguing with you, is there? You are a very determined man, and obviously used to having your own way."

"You betcha. Like I said, I like to win." Will's eyes spar-

kled with amusement. He seemed to thrive on the banter
that passed between them. Marty liked the way he made her
feel: young and silly, but attractive and desirable at the
same time. It was a heady combination.

When Will finally paid the bill and they left, Marty decided to be very bold. She waited until Will started the car.
"Next time," she declared, taking for granted that there
would be a next time, "dinner is on me."

"Don't be silly," Will said. "There is absolutely no
reason for you to buy me dinner."

"Of course there is. I enjoy your company, and it's my
turn to treat you." She crossed her arms over her chest, and
bounced slightly in her seat, signaling clearly that she would
not stand for any argument.

Will glanced at her determined profile out of the corner
of his eye. "All right," he said. "It seems to me that you're
pretty used to getting your own way, too."

Marty's mouth twitched with suppressed laughter. Not
because she thought it was funny, but because she felt such
immense relief that he had tacitly agreed there would be a
next time. Now all she had to do was come up with some
wonderful place to take him.

Will pulled to the curb in front of Marty's house, and
shut off the engine. Panic turned her legs to jelly. Did he
expect her to invite him in? She told herself she had no desire to repeat the adolescent necking of the previous evening. The truth was, she didn't trust herself to stop as she
had the night before. Will excited her in a way she had
never known possible, but she didn't want a quick affair.
That had never been her style. She was learning to relax
and enjoy the ride, but this was one route she wasn't ready
to take yet.

Her hesitancy seemed to communicate itself to Will. He

sat still, his arm draped over the steering wheel, half-turned to face her.

"You're really something," he said. "You seem to fit in wherever you go; elegant or casual. That's a pretty good talent to have."

"It's a necessary part of being in sales, actually. You learn to adapt. But I enjoy both. The company is what makes the real difference." Marty was amazed at her own boldness.

Will turned a bit more in his seat, and reached across to take her hand. "I'm glad you feel that way. I do too." Marty felt a tingle run up her arm and spread across her body. "Thanks for making this a fun evening." He grinned at her. "And you sing a pretty good 'Happy Birthday.' Remind me I should have you along for my next one."

At that he dropped her hand and came around to open her door. They went up the front walk hand in hand, Marty's heart hammering. Was it in fear, or anticipation? She wasn't sure, any more than she was sure what she would do when they got to the door.

On the tiny porch, she fumbled in her purse for her key, then turned to face Will, her key in her hand. He took the key from her, startling her with the gesture, and unlocked the door, then handed it back to her.

Without speaking, he took her in his arms, and held her close to him. His body was warm and oddly comforting, with no hint of the passion of the previous night.

She leaned her head on his chest for a moment, amazed at how well she seemed to fit in his arms. Not too short, after all. Then she pulled back to look up into his face. His arms tightened slightly around her, and he pulled her up onto her toes, gently touching her lips with his own. The kiss lingered quietly and softly, affectionate and undemanding. Marty finally broke the spell, once again leaning her head on his chest.

She caught a whiff of his fragrance, the smell she could only describe as Will, the smell that seemed so undeniably *right*.

"I really do have to work early tomorrow," she whispered. She was afraid of what his answer would be. She wanted him to stay, wanted him to overrule her restraint with his passion and desire. Wanted to surrender herself to the flame he had ignited within her. But it was too soon, her feelings for Will were too new. She wasn't ready to make a commitment, and she knew it.

Reluctantly, she drew herself from Will's arms. He gave a tiny groan of disappointment, but surrendered his hold on her. Backing away, she held his hand, stretching their arms out between them.

"It was wonderful," she said, still whispering. "Good night." And she slipped in the door, closing it quietly behind her.

She didn't turn on the light inside, but just leaned her back against the closed door, aware of Will's presence just on the other side. All she would have to do would be to open the door, and he would be there, holding her, kissing her, sweeping aside her objections.

She longed to do it, to pull the door slightly ajar and see his dear face, to swing the door wide and press him to her and drink in his musk. She closed her eyes, savoring again the feel of his lips so soft on hers, the warmth and power of his arms around her. He was tall, so tall that he had nearly pulled her off her feet when he kissed her, but they seemed to fit together as if they had been made for each other. Butterflies danced through her stomach at the memory.

She stood with her back to the door, summoning reserves of self-control. She could not open that door, it was too soon. But, oh, how she wished he would drive away, remove the temptation to throw caution and sense to the winds.

Please, she begged silently, please take your beautiful, fragrant, charming, *tempting* self away from here. Save me, just this once.

She could hear the Adams clock ticking on the curio shelf in the living room. It counted off the seconds as she forced herself to stay still.

She listened, counting the seconds, as it ticked off a minute, then two, then three. She still didn't hear Will's car start. Oh, lord, was he still standing out there, waiting? Did he know the turmoil she was in, was he waiting to see if she would change her mind? Trembling, she pushed herself away from the door.

Still wearing her jacket and carrying her purse, she crept to the window. Edging aside the curtain, she peered out into the darkness. In the pool of brightness from the porch light, she could see that the porch was empty.

As her eyes adjusted to the dark, she made out the figure of a man sitting in the driver's seat of Will's car. She imagined that she could see his eyes turned toward the window, could see him looking at her. Shaken and confused, she dropped the curtain as though it was aflame.

She heard the engine start then, and peeked out again in time to see tail lights as he pulled away from the curb. A sharp pang of disappointment and relief washed through her, and she sat heavily on the sofa in the dark, trying to decide which was the stronger.

Chapter 18

George Lane smashed an overhand shot at Will. It flew past him and ricocheted off the far wall. "Game, set, and match," George called, lowering his racquet. "You are definitely off your game today, buddy."

Will knew his game was off. He was having trouble concentrating on the ball, when his thoughts kept straying. His focus was not on his tennis game, but on a cute redhead that blushed and laughed. It was a strange and unsettling sensation.

George walked around the net, and clapped Will on the shoulder. "Where are you today, Will? It's certainly not on the tennis court."

Will shrugged. He knew his head wasn't in the game.

"Is it because I brought up Karen? Listen, man, I didn't mean to get in your face about it, I just thought you might be getting weirded out by working on that house."

In the locker room, the two men quickly showered, changed, and dropped their laundry bags off with the attendant. As they walked out the door, Will checked his watch. The plumber was due at eight, but he had a few minutes.

"Got time for coffee?" he asked.

George glanced at the time and nodded. "My morning's free. Downtown?"

Will shook his head. "How about the U District? I have a plumber due at eight. Maybe you'd like to see what I've done with the house?"

George shrugged. "Sure. I'll just drive through and meet you at the house. That all right?"

Will nodded, and climbed into his car. It was better, actually. This way he wouldn't have to worry about being late to meet the plumber and his helper. He hated wasting the time of his subs, especially when he was paying for it.

Pulling up in front of the house, Will was startled by how little had changed on the front. The trellises were attractive, but the rose bushes were bare. The only bright spots were the planters of mums by the front porch.

Still, he knew that when spring came runners would climb the trellises, and cover the front of the house with pale pink blossoms, the bulbs along the foundation would flower, and the ground cover would disguise the porch.

Will hadn't been past here in years, and he had been puzzling over what felt so wrong about the front yard. Now it came back to him.

There had been a large oak tree in the middle of the lawn when he and Karen had lived there. It was gone now, and he had no idea when or why. Too bad, too. It had shaded the front windows, making the house cooler in the summer heat.

George pulled up behind Will, and climbed out, his coffee in his hand. He took in the changes in the front yard, and nodded. "Looks better," he said, but there wasn't much enthusiasm in his voice.

"Come on inside," Will said, unlocking the door. "There are a few more things for you to see."

George was suitably impressed with the work Will had done. As they walked through the living room and dining room, he commented on the progress.

But he stopped when they reached the master bedroom. The room was crammed with the boxes containing the bathroom fixtures, and George stood and stared.

"O-kay. Just what is this?"

"Kitchens and bathrooms, the lady said. These are for the bathroom." He gestured through the open door.

George followed Will's gesture with his eyes. He stepped through the doorway, then let out a sharp laugh. "What a mess!"

Will laughed. "Don't I know it. That's why there's a plumber coming this morning. There is no way I can get that tub out, much less get the rest of the fixtures in, without help."

George looked back at Will, who tried to maintain a nonchalant posture. Then George snorted. "Aw, hell. I don't have anything going this morning, and I owe you for the drubbing you took at the club."

George set down his coffee and pulled off his jacket. "Let's see if we can't get that cabinet in place before the plumber gets here."

"You sure?" Will was already reaching for his tools, and tossing a pair of heavy work gloves to George.

"No. But I never could resist your hare-brained schemes."

They carefully leveled the cabinet and attached it to the stringers. In some strange way, it reminded Will of their college days, working odd hours to pay for books and tuition. It felt good to be getting his hands dirty again.

George leaned against the wall, panting. "I had forgotten how much *work* this is," he said.

Will grinned at him. "It comes back to you real fast. Especially the sore muscles part."

"But I'm *in shape*," George replied.

"That's what I thought." Will sank a final screw and crawled out from inside the cabinet, just as the doorbell rang. He glanced at his watch, and headed down the hall. "Right on time," he called back to George.

He greeted Bruce and his son, Terry, and led them back to the bathroom. "I appreciate you taking this on with such short notice. Since the auto shop job was delayed . . ." He shrugged. "I know residential isn't your usual thing, but this is a favor for a friend. Thanks for helping out."

"Not at all." Bruce read the markings on the fixture cartons and gave a low whistle. "Quite a favor, if you ask me. Remind me to charge you premium for this job."

Will chuckled. Bruce did a lot of work for him, and he was always more than fair with him. And he was one of the best. That never hurt.

It took most of the morning, two more coffee runs, and a colorful string of curses from George, but the tub was finally in place. The toilet was much simpler, and by lunchtime Bruce and Terry left, heading for another job.

Will and George left, too, to find a quick burger.

"I need to go home and clean up," George said, looking down at his sweatshirt. It was covered with dust and caulk, and there was a rip where he had caught the sleeve on a loose nail.

Will nodded. "Me too. There's a pile of stuff waiting at the office." He took another bite of his hamburger, and chewed for a moment.

"You know, George," he said, "I think you were right, the house was weirding me out. For a long time I thought I was over it, but being there reminded me of a lot.

"But the more I change the place, the less it reminds me of Karen. At this rate, it'll be just another house by next

146

month." Will stopped and made a face, as though trying to dismiss the serious thoughts he had just voiced. "Hell, if I keep this up, it *will* be another house by next month."

George gave his sharp laugh, and ate a handful of fries. "It nearly is already. I couldn't believe you had that entire back wall replaced with patio doors."

"Just wait," Will said. "There's going to be a garden outside the bathroom, with windows all around the tub. The windows and trim will be delivered next week." He gave George a look that said clearly he was invited to help install the windows.

"Oh, no you don't," George said quickly. "I'm almost sure I have to be out of town. All week. Absolutely."

"Sure," Will answered dryly. "Just as soon as you get to the office and schedule a trip."

"Hey, I never got past manual labor and rough framing. You don't want me anywhere near a window, at least not one made of glass."

Will grinned and gathered up the debris from their fast-food lunch, dropping it in the waste container on their way out. "We'll see, George. We'll see."

Chapter 19

Will stood back and admired his progress. The tub was in place, and he had mostly recovered from his adolescent fantasies about Marty. Still, he had to smile occasionally as he imagined her reaction to the work he had done.

George had capitulated, of course, and helped him with the garden window. Between the two of them, it had been one long afternoon, but the window was in place, and the exterior trim had been replaced.

In the bedroom, the sliders were in place, and he had some trim work to complete. When the trim was done, he would hang the blinds that complemented the new paint, and call it good. The rest would be up to the new owner.

He had reached the point that he no longer needed the van to haul materials and equipment, and he had celebrated the fall sunshine by riding his motorcycle, which he had parked in the alley.

It was time to finish up, and let go of the house. When he started the project, he had told himself it was for John and Betty, nothing more. After weeks of part-time work, he knew it had been for him, too. And for Karen.

He could think of Karen now without the catch in his stomach that had been his response for so many years. It was time he thought about his future, instead of filling his days with his job and his company, and locking out his past.

He was beginning to wonder if that future might hold a certain redhead, one who seemed to invade his thoughts, no matter where he went or what he did.

He was anxious to finish. He wanted to see Marty's face when he walked her through the house, and showed her the things he had done. He was proud of his work, a pride that was far different, more private and personal, than what he felt when a building topped out, or a project was completed.

He had had fun doing this house, and he would look for another one when this one sold. There was something satisfying about the process of restoring a house that had been neglected, bringing it back as a warm, inviting home. Something deeply rewarding about doing the work himself.

At least the next time, and he was sure there would be a next time, he would know where the pitfalls were, and how to avoid them. Next time, he would make a whole new bunch of mistakes.

Will went out through the sliding doors into the back yard. He had put up a tall fence around the garden window, following the line of the window. It divided the patio slab, providing a private area off the master bedroom.

Inside the fence, he had started work on the flower garden that would be visible from the tub. He had cut away the sod, and filled the area back in with planting mix. He glanced through the tall gate, and considered what to tackle next. There were bulbs to plant for spring, and some evergreen bushes to provide some green through the winter. He planned to drag one pot of mums around from the front porch, and there was a replacement on order at the nursery. Next time he would remember to do the landscaping before the approaching winter limited his options.

The sun had dropped behind the tall trees in the neighbor's yard, sending cool shadows across the back yard. Will considered for a moment, then decided to walk the two blocks to Java Jungle for hot coffee before he tackled the garden.

He might even stop and have a muffin. He'd been working hard, and he deserved a reward.

Marty remembered very little about the events of her date, but she remembered everything about Will. The way he held his head when he listened—really listened—to what she said. The tiny scar on the back of his right hand, nearly hidden beneath the crisp blond hair. How he ate his ice cream, carefully portioning out the hot fudge so that there would be some in every spoonful. That he drank iced tea with real sugar. All the little details that she examined over and over.

She sat at her desk, and tried to push the thought of Will from her mind. She had work to do, and it did not include mooning over some impossibly attractive handyman.

Ralph Gordon walked into the office like he owned the place. He didn't bother to stop at the receptionist, but simply walked up to Marty's desk, dropped his briefcase, and headed for the coffee pot. Marty sighed. She liked Ralph, though she had pushed him, and his gift, to the back of her mind the last few days. But now, now that there was Will, how would she feel about his teasing?

Ralph dropped into her visitor's chair, and waved his coffee cup at her. "How goes the hunt? Have you found anything I can't live without? Besides you, that is."

Much to her relief, Marty felt no change in her reaction to Ralph. She laughed at him, and felt the easy banter come unforced. "You've made it this far without me, Ralph. I figure you're good for at least a few more years."

"Don't be so sure about that. I'm getting old, and it just

may be too much for me before long." His eyes strayed to the credenza behind her, and a shadow passed across them as he caught sight of her briefcase, her *old* briefcase, sitting open on the top. "But I'll try to bear up under the disappointment." His voice was light, but Marty felt an undertone of rebuke, a touch of hurt at her continuing refusal to use his gift.

"You're not that old," Marty chided him. "Besides, some of us just have trouble making up our minds. You have to give us time."

Though she kept the same bantering tone, she hoped he would understand the second layer of meaning beneath her words. She had accepted the gift under duress, and she still hadn't decided what it would mean, to her and to Ralph, if she actually used it. Until she did, she still wanted to have the option of returning it to him.

"All right, have it your way. I'm not that old. But I am still disappointed." He waved away her anticipated retort, and straightened in the chair, his face changing from an expression of give-and-take to one of down-to-business. "Since you aren't going to fall into my arms, we might as well get to work here. Got anything I might like?"

Marty slid the multiple-listing book toward him. "I'm not really supposed to let you have this, but why don't you just take a look for yourself? I have a couple things in mind, including one in the same neighborhood as that one on Agate that we saw."

"Yeah, I remember that one," Ralph said, lifting the book into his lap and setting his coffee cup on the desk. "What did the guy ever decide to do to it?"

"He's ripped up the master bedroom and bathroom, and put the sliders in, like you suggested. I think it's going to look pretty good when he gets it done."

"Hmmm," Ralph was already deep into the book, not seeming to pay attention to her reply, but he looked up for a second. "Might like to see how it turned out," he said, before going back to reading.

It was three-quarters of an hour before Marty and Ralph left the office. They stopped for a fast-food burger, and discussed the houses each had selected for the afternoon's touring. Marty had included the house in the Agate neighborhood, and Ralph had one near the university that he thought might fit him. They settled on a route, and set out. The subject of the briefcase was never brought up, almost as though they had agreed not to talk about it.

Ralph was disappointed in the university-area house, and they were dismayed to find another agent writing up an offer on the house near Will's. None of the others had quite fit either, and they were about to call it quits for the day, when Marty asked if Ralph wanted to see the work at the Agate house.

"I think I would," Ralph answered. He was sitting in the passenger seat of her car. "I'm disappointed in what we did see—this seems to be my day for disappointment," he grinned briefly, as though trying to take the sting out of his words, "and maybe that will make me feel better."

"Let's go take a look," Marty said. "I'd hate for you to go home thinking the day was a total loss." She returned his grin, but it took an effort.

Her own disappointment was wearing on her. There was still the sales contest, and the holidays were coming. She could expect sales to slow down, and her expenses always got a little out of control, despite her annual resolution to set limits on her holiday spending.

Marty parked the car in the driveway on Agate. She looked briefly at the single-car garage in front of her. None of her prospects had even gotten that far, and she wondered idly whether there was anything worthwhile in it. She shrugged, and went in the house with Ralph. She hadn't seen the garage, and she wouldn't bother to today. She didn't care enough to look.

Something was different about the living room. She realized it had been repainted, a delicate off-white with a slight undertone of yellow. It seemed to pull in the pale afternoon light and amplify it, making the room seem larger and more open. The color continued down the hall to the bedrooms.

In the master bedroom, the transformation was nearly complete. The sliding doors were in place, opening the room to the light and the space of the backyard. A garden window had replaced the back wall of the bathroom, extending out from the back of the house and creating the feeling of privacy on the concrete patio slab outside the sliding doors. There were strips of molding waiting to cover the exposed edges of the doors, and Marty could see boxes of mini-blinds stacked in the closet, ready to be hung when the construction was finished.

They walked through into the master bath, admiring the spacious feeling that came from the garden window at the end of the room. Through the window they could see the mounds of newly-turned soil and mulch, waiting for the addition of landscaping, surrounded by the privacy fence which completed the exterior portion of the room.

But the crowning touch was already in place. Sunk into the floor in the alcove created by the window, was an over-sized jetted tub glazed a deep shade of forest green, accented by gleaming brass hardware. The tile surrounding the tub was stark white, with occasional accents of the same green as the tub. Marty gasped involuntarily at the luxurious display. Ralph whistled softly.

"I'd say the guy took you real serious, darlin'."

"But . . . I just told him kitchens and bathrooms, and to let some light in. I had no idea . . ." She turned to examine the rest of the room, taking in the new sink and vanity; the basin of the same forest green and brass, the vanity top was a seamless expanse of white, with a backsplash of white and green tile that followed the design surrounding the tub.

Finally she turned to face Ralph. "It's spectacular, isn't it? But I am so afraid he's overbuilding. This neighborhood just isn't quite . . ." She seemed at a loss to describe just what it was that the neighborhood wasn't. "I hope that this area will be the next place to be 'discovered,' that the houses around here will be the next target for rehabbing. I think it's going to happen, but I'm just not sure when. I don't know if it's a good gamble to put this much work into a house around here quite yet."

She wondered how much this had cost Will, whether she would ever be able to get a price that would justify the work he had done. Some of this must have been done by professionals, of that she was certain.

"It's great, Marty. Whoever did this had a great sense of style, and a feel for class and quality. The materials are top-notch, and look at the work." He walked to the edge of the tub, and started pointing out details of the tile work. She followed him back into the bedroom, as he continued to show her telling details in the installation of the sliders. Nodding, she continued to follow him as they walked back down the hall to the living room, and through to the dining room.

Ralph stopped her with a hand on her arm as they walked through the open doorway between the living and dining rooms. "I really like what's going on here." He waved his arm, encompassing all the work that had been done. "I think I just might be interested, after all. But there is still the question of a token of appreciation that hasn't been settled."

"Ralph!" Marty was startled by the bluntness of his approach, after he had let the subject slide earlier. "I told you, I just can't accept anything like that."

"And I told you there were no strings attached. Unless," his voice dropped slightly, and his hand slipped up her arm to rest on her shoulder, "you want there to be."

"I, um, I don't think so, Ralph. You're sweet, and we've always been friends. I don't want to spoil that." She reached up and rested her fingers lightly on Ralph's chin. "Really, I'm just not ready to get involved."

"Well, when you are, remember me, would you?"

Marty nodded, and Ralph kissed her lightly on the forehead. She was about to protest, when she heard the squeak of a rubber-soled shoe on the kitchen floor. Turning, she saw the back of a familiar dark head pass out the back door.

She ran for the kitchen door, unsure what Will might have seen, or heard. Where had he come from? What was he doing there? And what must he be thinking, seeing her in *this* house, in what could be taken as an intimate moment with Ralph?

From the kitchen window she saw him pull open the side door of the garage, and by the time she reached the kitchen door she could hear the engine of a motorcycle roaring to life.

Before she could reach the garage, the motorcycle had shot down the alley, and he was gone. She stood in the backyard, staring sightlessly at the bare branches of an apple tree. The warmth of her friendship with Ralph had faded and her veins felt as though they were filled with ice water. Gloom settled over her, matching the growing overcast of the late October afternoon.

She walked back to the kitchen and let herself into the house.

Ralph met her at the back door. He looked at her, eyebrows raised in question.

"That," she said, "was the man who's working on the house. The man," she added with a sigh, "that I had dinner with two nights in a row last week. The one I invited for a special Halloween dinner, tomorrow night."

"Oh." The single syllable carried Ralph's regret, embarrassment, and understanding. He carefully locked the back door, and led Marty through the house. She locked up, and they drove back to the office in silence.

After she parked the car, Ralph turned to her, a rueful smile on his face. "I hope I didn't mess things up back there. He may not know it yet, but he's a lucky guy." Then he was gone, jumping into his Jeep Cherokee and squealing out of the parking lot.

Great. Two men in her life, and in one day they both high-tailed it away from her, burning rubber like a couple of show-off high-schoolers. Just what she needed. That should remind her why she didn't need *any* man in her life, they always seemed to be playing these kind of adolescent games. She was better off alone.

So why did she feel like burying her head in her hands and crying?

Will sat in the noisy coffee shop, a cup of plain black coffee warming his hands. The place was full of students, their backpacks slung over the backs of mismatched chairs, as informal study groups gathered around scarred tables. It hadn't changed much from when Will was a student.

Except that he couldn't afford this place when he was a student. Then he had scraped for every nickel, studying at the kitchen table of his rented house, and drinking whatever kind of coffee was on sale. He was reminded again of the gift John Baker had given him, when he pulled him aside and suggested Will consider returning to school.

Which brought him back to the house. It was waiting for its new garden, and trim on the sliding doors, and those things weren't going to get done on their own.

A creeping grayness was taking over the sky. He had better get back and finish up what he could before the weather got any worse—he couldn't put it off until tomorrow. He wouldn't be able to work on it tomorrow.

As he walked the two blocks back, and turned up the alley to go in the back yard, he went over his plans for the next day. He didn't have to look at his notebook, though it was safely in his pocket, as always.

There was a full day tomorrow, visiting job sites and checking for end of month progress billings, as well as another payroll. And his evening was spoken for.

He had already picked up the movies he'd told Marty he would bring. She had promised him dinner, and refused his offer to bring a bottle of wine. "This is my turn, remember? Just bring yourself, and the movies."

He was looking forward to dinner. It had been a long time since someone had cooked for him.

It was strange to think about, but he hadn't really dated in years. He went out, to civic affairs and community events, but when he took a companion it was always business. Even his "dates" were business acquaintances—women he worked with, or who served on various committees with him.

He wondered what those women would think of him now, in faded denims, his flannel shirt spattered with tile grout, and his boots stained with the soil of the new garden. Some of them, he was sure, wouldn't even recognize him.

Even the ones who saw him on job sites were used to crisply pressed shirts and slacks. They wouldn't know the grubby handyman that walked into the Bakers' back yard.

There was a light on in the kitchen. He grimaced. Someone had come by, even though he'd had George note on the listing that there was work in progress. Well, it had probably killed another sale, if what Marty said was right.

Will shrugged. There would be other buyers, and in the next few days the place would come together, and they wouldn't be able to resist it. No harm, no foul.

Still, it might be a good idea to go in and explain.

Will slid his key into the back door. He felt a tiny surge of pride when the door swung open easily and quietly. Like the rest of the doors, he had oiled the hinges and reset all the locks.

He walked through the laundry room, and stopped in the doorway into the kitchen. In front of him, framed by the doorway into the dining room, was a picture he didn't want to see. But it was already burned into his memory.

He didn't know the man, but he could spot those red curls from across the street, much less across the kitchen. Marty stood still, her hand resting against the man's face, a caress that spoke of an intimacy Will didn't want to think about.

The man was tall, though not as tall as Will. He had his hand on Marty's shoulder, and he was kissing her forehead. There was a possessive quality in the way he touched her, a familiarity in his relaxed posture. Clearly, he knew her well.

For one interminable moment, Will couldn't move. All he could do was stare.

What was she doing here? What were *they* doing here? And what kind of a fool had he been?

They obviously hadn't seen him, caught up in whatever

they were doing. Will moved then, turning to leave the way he had come. He just wanted to get away before they knew he was there, before he had to confront them.

The heavy rubber sole of his boot squeaked against the tile on the floor, but he didn't stop. Three long strides took him out the door, and he hurried across the lawn to the side door of the garage, and into the alley.

Without looking back, he threw his leg across the motor-cycle. The engine roared to life, and he rode down the alley, and onto the street.

All the way home, Will replayed the scene in his mind. He wasn't sure what exactly he had seen, but it was clear to him that there was someone in Marty's life, someone who had been around for much longer than he had, by the looks of it.

He parked the bike in the garage, and took the elevator to his condo. He considered his options while he showered. While he waited for a microwave dinner to heat, he tried to decide what to do about tomorrow night's dinner.

By the time he had eaten, and laid out a specifications for a bid that needed his attention, he had a plan.

Will knew he had no claim on Marty, and maybe he had read more into her responses than she had intended. After their initial clinch, she had kept him safely at arm's length. She had given him no real reason to assume that they were more than friends.

He wanted to believe the man he'd seen was intruding on his budding relationship with Marty. But he had to admit it was more likely that he was the intruder, and he should back off. It wouldn't be easy, but it was the honorable thing to do.

Will sighed, and turned his attention to his work. Why was it that the right thing to do was sometimes the hardest?

Chapter 20

Standing in the living room, Marty looked around her, checking one more time that things were ready. Everything was done, just waiting for Will to arrive—that was assuming Will showed up. After yesterday, she didn't know what to expect.

When Ralph left, Marty had gone back into the office, and worked the last hour or so on auto pilot. She kept hoping the phone would ring, that Will would call and give her the chance to explain. By five-thirty everyone had gone, and Dotty was cleaning up to leave. When she turned the phones over to the service for the evening, Marty gave up and went home.

She was afraid to stop at the grocery store, in case Will might call her at home, as he had taken to doing in the last few days. But there were no messages on the machine, and the only call she had all evening was from Beth.

"I don't know what happened," she told her best friend. "Ralph and I were in the neighborhood, and he wanted to see how the work was going. We stopped and looked at the house, and he made a pass . . ."

"But he always makes a pass, and you always shut him down. That should have been clear to anyone. What was different about this?"

"It's hard to say. It didn't feel like as much of a joke this time. It's like he was serious, and I tried to be honest with him. I told him that I wasn't ready to get involved with anyone. He seemed to take it okay, and he kissed me on the forehead, like I was his kid sister or something. And right about that time I heard somebody in the kitchen, and I turned around in time to see Will go out the back door, fire up a motorcycle, and take off down the alley. He was gone before I could get to him, and he hasn't called since."

"So why don't you call him?"

"Beth, I have never called a man in my life. Except for business, of course. I can't do it."

Beth chuckled at her friend. "Honey, that attitude went out with poodle skirts, and you aren't that old. But never mind. Aren't you supposed to have dinner tomorrow?"

Marty sighed into the phone and explained her plans to Beth, for the third time.

"Then wait and see what he does. Same old advice, hon, relax and see what happens."

What happens, Marty thought, plucking a miniature Baby Ruth bar from the bowl of candy by the front door, is he doesn't show up, and I've wasted a perfectly good dinner on a jerk.

That wasn't fair, and she knew it. Will wasn't a jerk, although he certainly wasn't making this easy on her. A simple phone call was all she asked. No, she hadn't called him, and she wouldn't. But why couldn't he call her?

She checked the Adams clock, and her watch—just in case the clock was wrong. They both agreed that it was six-fifteen.

She had told Will six-thirty. They had planned an early dinner and a couple old horror movies, 'in the spirit of the season,' Will had said, and Marty had groaned delightedly at the horrid pun. Now she was pacing, waiting for she wasn't sure what.

Every time the doorbell rang, she jumped. And each time she opened the door to witches and ghosts, fairy princesses and super heroes. "Trick or treat!" they shouted. She dropped candy in their outstretched bags and pails, and listened to mumbled "thank-yous" as they ran for the next house.

The bell rang, and she ran again. There was a group of five or six children, the youngest one only about three years old. The older ones got their candy and ran off, leaving the little one standing, slightly bewildered, on Marty's porch. She crouched down, putting their faces on a level, and held out a candy bar to him. "Would you like your treat?" she asked in a soft voice. He nodded, looking too overwhelmed to speak.

She smiled, and reached to drop the candy into his plastic jack o'lantern pail. The little boy managed to stammer a "thank-you" as his mother came up behind him, and took him by the hand. With his mother's reassuring presence, he rewarded Marty with a wide grin, and trotted down the walk.

She started to straighten up, and found a large, square hand thrust in front of her. "Trick or treat," said the familiar, teasing voice, sending a rush of relief through her.

He had showed up.

She had been so distracted by the children that she hadn't heard his car, or seen him come striding up the walk in the dark.

He took her hand and steadied her as she stood up. She thought it was probably a good thing he did, her knees felt like spaghetti noodles, and she wasn't sure she could have stood without his help. Without letting go of his hand, she met his eyes. His expression was bland, giving away nothing of his feelings. She wished she could tell what was on his mind, but she would just have to wait it out.

"Hi," she said, relieved that her voice, at least, was steady. "Come on in."

She led him through the front door, suddenly aware that this was the first man she had let into her house since she'd moved in.

"It's not much, but it's home and it's mine," she apologized. She saw the room as he must: a small, square room crowded with a futon sofa, a glass-topped cocktail table and matching end tables, thrift store lacquered bookcases, bright yellow ginger-jar lamps, her beat-up papasan chair, and an imitation oak-veneer entertainment center.

She didn't want him to know how proud she was of the last item. It had been an assemble-it-yourself piece, packed in two giant cardboard boxes. She'd had Ken help her lug the boxes in after work one day, and then she'd put it all together by herself. She'd even figured out how to put casters underneath it, so that she could move it by herself.

She had tried to soften the sharp edges and the "budget" styling of the furniture with living greenery. Pots of well-tended and carefully trimmed plants stood on the tables and atop the bookcases. African violets spread across the top of the entertainment center, and an avocado tree, sprouted from a seed many years before, stood in the corner of the room.

Through the doorway, the dining room was visible. It was rather a grandiose description for what had once been an overly large pantry. Before Marty bought the house, it had been opened into the kitchen and a built-in dining nook installed. Now the table was set with a red and white checkered tablecloth, and her best dishes. Wine glasses had been polished until they gleamed, and the basket of breadsticks had taken her twenty minutes to arrange exactly the way she wanted.

Hesitantly, Marty beckoned Will to follow her. "I was just getting ready to put the pasta in to boil when the doorbell rang," she said, as she passed through the doorway and turned right, into the kitchen proper.

The pot of spaghetti sauce was simmering on a back burner, thickened to the point that it erupted in tiny volcanic explosions from time to time. On the front burner, water bubbled furiously. The long spaghetti noodles that Marty preferred were sitting on the counter next to the stove.

"Something smells fantastic," Will said, as he stood in the kitchen watching her. She poured a little olive oil in the boiling water and added the spaghetti, nudging it further into the water as it softened. Once it was boiling again to her satisfaction, she turned to face Will.

"I hope breadsticks are all right with you. By the time I got to the store this afternoon they were out of French bread, so I couldn't make garlic bread to go with the spaghetti."

"Breadsticks are fine. Sometimes I actually prefer them." Marty wasn't sure whether to believe him, but she appreciated that he tried to put her at ease.

Their attempt at conversation was broken up by the doorbell. Marty trotted past Will to answer it, and distribute candy to the group of three small astronauts that appeared. Will wandered around the kitchen, stopping where he could see her, and watch her with the children.

When she returned, he could see the amusement twinkling in her eyes. "They are so cute, every one of them. The tiny ones are the cutest, of course. Just before you got here, there was this one little guy—he was dressed up as a dino-saur, in a costume that must have taken his mother hours to make. Anyway, he rang the bell, and when I answered he said, 'Hi' and walked right in! I started laughing, he was just so bold, and sure of himself. He couldn't have been more than two or three, and he was just precious! His mother grabbed his little green dinosaur tail, and pulled him back out, but he didn't seemed fazed by it at all."

Will laughed with her, amused by her story. They talked while she finished cooking, and once, while she was stirring the sauce, Will hurried to the summons of the bell and doled out candy to the small witches who begged for treats. It felt so right to have him there, to be so *domestic* together. Marty served dinner, and they shared the bottle of Chianti Will had brought, despite her protests.

When they had eaten their fill, Will pushed himself back from the table with a groan. "Any more, and I'll be spending *two* hours a night at the gym. It was delicious." He raised his glass, as he had on their first date. "To a beautiful lady, and a great cook. Your talents never cease to amaze me."

Marty's cheeks burned as she drank. Will helped her stack the dishes, and they settled on the sofa with the rest of the wine. Will put one of the tapes he'd brought in the VCR, and pushed the Play button. A black-and-white Universal logo appeared on the screen, and the credits for *The Mummy* appeared, chiseled onto a slowly-revolving pyramid.

"Hope this is okay," Will said. "I have a weakness for these old horror flicks, and Halloween seems like the perfect night for them."

Marty sat next to him on the sofa, but didn't crowd him. He had been cheerful and relaxed all evening, but there had been an undercurrent of reserve. He had made no attempt to embrace her, or kiss her, but had limited their contact to the hand-holding that had happened when he arrived.

She watched the movie, and waited for him to make the first move. When at last the Boris Karloff's mummy was vanquished, and Helen Chandler was saved from a fate worse than death, Will stretched as the tape was rewinding, and asked where her bathroom was. She showed him the door down the short hall, next to the two bedroom doors.

While he was gone, she tidied up the empty glasses and bottle, and put on a kettle to boil. She didn't want coffee this late in the evening, but maybe Will would join her for a cup of herbal tea, or some cocoa. As she laid out cups and spoons, she heard him change tapes.

The trick-or-treaters had stopped early in the movie, and the street outside was quiet. It seemed so odd, and yet so right, to have Will in the house, her house, with her.

This had been her place alone; Charlie had never lived here, and she had kept it as a refuge during the long months of rebuilding her life and her self-esteem. Now, hearing Will moving around in the living room, she realized that she was ready to share her life with another person. She was ready to share her life with Will.

She stuck her head around the corner of the door, and found him staring at the titles in her bookshelf. "I'm a terrible packrat when it comes to books," she said by way of explanation. "I hate to get rid of any of them, so I have what can best be described as an eclectic collection there."

"You can tell a lot about someone by what books they read," he answered.

Marty hastily changed the subject. She guessed there were some things she wasn't so sure she was ready to share. "Would you care for a cup of tea, or cocoa? I don't usually

166

drink coffee at night, but I could make some for you if you want."

"No, tea would be fine."

"Regular or herbal?"

They decided on a pot of Ruby Mist, and Will carried the tray with teapot, mugs, and a plate of dainty sugar cookies into the living room. They sat back down on the sofa, a careful distance between them.

"So," Marty asked brightly, "what's the second half of our double feature?"

"*The Wolfman,*" Will answered, starting the tape. Marty settled back with her tea and a cookie, content for now to watch the movie.

"I don't think I had ever seen that all the way through," Marty said when it was done. "Must be something lacking in my popular culture education."

Will was fiddling with the tapes and their cases, putting them back in the bag from the video store. "Glad I was able to fill the gap," he said. He put the bag by the door. "I better remember to drop these off on my way home. I rented them two days ahead, just to be sure I got what I wanted."

Marty had been waiting all evening for him to bring up the subject of Ralph, and the scene he had witnessed the night before. But Will was getting his coat from the tree by the door, and it was obvious that he was ready to leave.

She couldn't let it go like this, without trying to explain what had happened. She didn't want the evening to end with the same polite but distant tone.

He was putting on his coat, when she touched his arm. "Will, about yesterday."

He looked at her, then continued to shrug his shoulders into the coat. He wasn't making this any easier.

She plunged ahead. "I just wanted a chance to talk to you about what happened."

Will put his hand on the doorknob, and looked at her. "There's no need to explain anything. A couple dates doesn't mean I own you, or that you owe me anything, any more than I need to explain my friends to you. I always assumed you had other friends, and I never expected that to change just because we had dinner a few times."

"But it isn't . . ."

"You don't owe me any explanations. All I ever asked for was the pleasure of your company. I got your company, and it was a pleasure." He leaned over and kissed her on the cheek, a gesture too painfully similar to the brotherly kiss Ralph had given her. "It's late. I have to go. I'll call you."

And he was gone. Down the walk, out to his car, the video bag dangling from his wrist as he opened the door. She saw the dome light come on, and watched him toss the bag on the passenger seat.

She wanted to run to him, to beg him to listen, to make him understand that there was nothing between her and Ralph. He was the one she wanted. But it seemed abundantly clear that he didn't want her, that she had been building a dream house in the clouds, and had nearly moved into it, making things up, only to find there was no one there to share it with.

She stood rooted by fear and humiliation to the spot where he had left her, staring out the partially open door, watching his tail lights fade into the fog. He turned the corner, and the lights were gone, leaving only the fog and the chill creeping in the door and up Marty's ankles.

When she finally noticed the cold, she closed the door gently, and cried herself to sleep in the cold, gray Halloween night.

Chapter 21

Marty moped through the next week at the office. She tried burying herself in her work. She spent extra hours poring over the multiple-listing books, and stayed late two evenings cleaning out her old files. By Thursday all her filing was current, her desk was immaculate—and she could feel that people were avoiding her.

Lorraine and Dotty approached Marty's desk, looking as though they should be waving a white flag. The concern on the two women's faces was genuine, and their worried expressions reminded Marty of how prickly she was being to the people around her. Usually she was the one who maintained an even keel, seeing all sides of an issue, and remaining calm and in control. Now she was snapping where she usually chatted, and snarling when she usually smiled.

Dotty sat in the visitor's chair, and Lorraine leaned one hip on the edge of the desk. It was Lorraine who took the lead.

"Marty, there is something horribly wrong here. You've been having a bad week of it, for some reason, and it's affecting the rest of us."

"Sorry," Marty said, with a sulky look that told the two of them that she wasn't in the least sorry. "I certainly didn't mean to taint the entire office with my problems."

"Oh, bull!" It was as close to swearing as anyone had

ever heard Dotty get. Marty glanced up at her, and caught the glint of tears in Dotty's eyes. "There is something really wrong, and it's about time that you opened up and at least let us try to help.

"You helped me through that mess with Craig, and stood up for me with Jerry, but you won't let me help you. I may not be able to solve the problem, or change what's bothering you, but I'm a pretty good listener."

"It's obvious that something is bothering you," Lorraine took over, as Dotty compressed her lips and blinked rapidly. "You can't always keep it bottled up, no matter how hard you try."

Lorraine leaned forward, forcing Marty to look at her. "We watched you through your divorce, and you wouldn't let anyone close. You kept it pretty quiet, even on the worst days. But whatever this is, it's got you flustered to the point that Ken noticed. He even asked me if I knew what the problem was."

"If there is some problem with my work, then let Ken speak to me about it," Marty said stiffly.

"It's not affecting your work," Lorraine answered. "At least, not yet. But if you keep going, you're headed for trouble."

"Please, Marty," Dotty had her voice back under control, "we just want to help."

Marty lowered her head into her hands. She sat without moving for two long minutes, while the other women waited patiently. At last she raised her eyes to them, and she knew they could see the tears threatening to overflow. "It's just such a stupid mess!"

"Can't be much worse than what I got myself into," Dotty replied briskly. "C'mon, let's go back in the conference room and see what we can figure out."

The three women sat at the conference table. Marty gave

them the highlights of the last few weeks with Will, carefully avoiding any mention of how their first date ended.

"You're really gone on this guy," Dotty summed up after listening to the ten-minute abridgment.

"I guess I am. But it doesn't seem like he feels the same way. I feel like such a prize jerk, and I haven't even been able to talk to Beth about it, because I half-way blame her for what happened. 'Relax,' she said. 'See where it goes.' " Marty wadded up the napkin she had been twisting into knots, and threw it violently into the wastebasket. "That's where it went, and I really didn't need the aggravation."

"Are you sure it's all that bad?" Lorraine asked. "I mean, it hasn't even been a week, and he might just be busy, or out of town, or something."

"I don't think so." Marty admitted that she had been past the Agate house nearly every night, hoping to find him there. She hadn't, but she did see the continuing work on the house, so she was sure he'd been there. Just not when she was around.

"Give it a few more days," was Lorraine's advice. "Let yourself get over the initial hurt, and try to get a little distance on it. Then call him. If he really isn't interested, he'll let you know."

"I can't." Marty felt miserable. "I can't give him another chance to push me away." She stood up and paced the length of the small room, her heels clicking on the hard tile floor. She was visibly pulling herself together, straightening her posture, and pulling her chin up. "But it's no excuse for messing up around here.

"Thanks for letting me talk this out, guys. I needed to get it off my chest, even if I didn't know it. I'll see to it that it doesn't happen again." She flashed a smile that was all teeth, and no eyes, and opened the conference room door.

"Better get back to the grind, before anyone decides they can get along without us."

As Marty walked down the corridor back to her desk, the two other women exchanged worried glances. The confident, cheerful, take-charge Marty was back, but at what cost, and for how long?

Their concern for Marty was quickly replaced, however, by the appearance of Jerry. It was an unusual day and time for him to be in the office, and the speculation started the minute he had closed his office door, after calling Velma and Ken in with him. The answers to everyone's questions were quick in coming.

"Ladies and gentlemen," Jerry spoke loudly, calling the buzzing office to attention. "You will all remember the unfortunate scene created by Mr. Sailors at his departure from this firm a few weeks ago." People nodded, and there was a murmured chorus of assent. "At that time, he made a rather dramatic exit, and said we hadn't heard the last of him. Today we found out exactly what he meant.

"This morning my lawyer was served with notice of a civil lawsuit filed by Mr. Sailors. He is charging the firm, and myself, Mr. Stocker, and Mrs. Little as individuals, with sexual discrimination and breach of contract."

There was a moment of stunned silence. Dotty crumpled in her chair. Clearly, she was sure her job would be gone after this latest challenge.

The rest of the staff reacted with outrage. One of the men jumped up so violently that he sent his office chair spinning across the floor. Lorraine, forgetting her image as the clown, shouted, "That bastard!"

Jerry shot her a look that somehow conveyed his thanks for saying what he couldn't.

Ken took over from Jerry. He spoke woodenly, as though

he had rehearsed the lines. "We had completed the assessment of the sales contest, and had come up with what we felt was a fair way of distributing the points that had been accumulated by Craig. Generally it involved awarding his sales points to the listing agent, and his listing points to the selling agent. Unsold listings would simply be considered a house listing, though there would be a consideration for selling one of these 'orphan' houses. We wanted to encourage everyone to continue showing the houses that Craig listed, instead of only those listings generated by the other members of the staff.

"For the moment, these plans have been placed on hold. The current contest standings are posted on the bulletin board. They do not reflect any distribution of Craig's points. We feel we must wait to do that until the matter of this lawsuit is settled." Ken perched one hip on the corner of a table, and looked expectantly at Jerry.

"We do not expect this suit to go very far. I am of the opinion, and my attorneys share this opinion, that Mr. Sailors is simply being vindictive, and his lawyer will soon find there is little legal merit to his arguments. That won't necessarily stop his lawyer from bringing suit, but I have a reasonable expectation that when he realizes how weak the case is, he will persuade his client to drop the suit before it ends up costing them both.

"In the meantime, just keep doing what you normally do. It will probably take at least a few weeks before this is settled, and we can't let it shut us down while we're taking care of it.

"Thank you for your time. We will keep you posted as things develop."

The three managers disappeared back into Jerry's office, but it was apparent they were watching the employees through the office windows.

Marty sat stiffly in her chair. She knew that she stood to gain the most from the proposed distribution scheme, since she had sold three or four of Craig's listings in the last month, and he had sold two of hers. It would be enough to put her firmly in the lead. But nothing could happen until the lawsuit was settled.

Besides, she reminded herself bitterly, what good was a cruise for two when you didn't have someone to go with you? She had somehow pictured herself and Will standing together at the rail, as the ship pulled out to sea. Her imagination had taken them to their luxurious cabin, where a basket of exotic fresh fruit awaited them, along with a perfectly chilled bottle of vintage champagne.

Now, even if she did win, she'd have to take Beth, and she knew they'd spend the week drinking diet sodas from the can and sharing tiny foil packets of complimentary cocktail peanuts.

The phone rang, and Marty pulled herself out of her daydream to answer it. Another couple referred by the Hortons, who wondered if the house on Agate was still available. Marty stiffened her spine, and made arrangements to show them the house that afternoon. By golly, if she couldn't have Will, at least she could sell his darned house and get him out of her life for good.

She made a note to send the Hortons a house plant as a thank-you gift, and headed for the door. Velma, Ken, and Jerry were still in Jerry's office, clustered around Jerry's desk, deep in conversation, one or another occasionally glancing up to check on the office as they talked.

Marty stuck her chin out and left the office. She didn't need any of Craig's points. She could win this contest on her own work.

She didn't need any man.

Chapter 22

Will sat at his desk, a payroll report and sub-contractor schedule spread in front of him. He carefully marked the labor hours he had used on the Bakers' house, along with the contractors' time and materials.

The total would be billed back as a personal draw against his earnings. It represented the final work on the house, and it had been worth it.

After Halloween, he had lost a certain amount of enthusiasm for the project. Despite his resolve, he had used some subs and crew when there were gaps in their schedules, and had pushed the job through.

He didn't want to examine too closely the reasons the project had lost its appeal. He told himself that he had put his memories to rest, and that was why he had let it go. It had stopped being personal.

It had nothing to do with the fantasies he had entertained of a certain redhead in a dark green bathtub.

Will glanced up at the window, startled at how quickly darkness had fallen across the building. The days were getting shorter, and the nights were colder. Winter was definitely on the way, the auto service center would be finished soon, and his business would slow down for the season.

It was time to decide what he would do during the slow

months. There were a couple small jobs, some indoor work, but he would have a lot of time on his hands in the coming months. He should figure out how he would use it.

Maybe it was time for a vacation. He loved San Diego in the winter, the clear skies and the warm sunshine. He had friends there to visit, and he could get in a little sailing.

But the thought of San Diego reminded him of his ice cream parlor date with Marty, and his promise to take her there. San Diego might not be such a great idea, after all.

Will initialed the totals of his charges, and set the stack of invoices and time cards on Rita's desk. She would take care of the rest of it on Monday.

He locked the door behind himself, and climbed into his pickup. Unable to come up with a better plan, he'd go home. Maybe he could find a football game on television. And he didn't even like football.

So this is what it's like to be an eligible bachelor.

Marty picked up the Franks at their motel, across from the university campus. When she pulled up, the couple was easy to spot. It was a football weekend, and they were the only people in the parking lot who weren't wearing the school colors of green and gold.

They were, however, wearing bewildered looks, as groups of blanket-toting fans passed by hollering, "Go, Ducks!"

Marty bundled them into the Lincoln, and introduced herself. As they drove to the house, she explained the mania that seemed to grip the entire town, as the football team posted a winning season for the first time in nearly two decades.

"You know how it is with a college town," she said.

Mrs. Frank nodded her understanding, but the apprehension did not leave her face until they crossed the invisible southern boundary that marked the edge of the university district.

As the neighborhood changed from frat houses and student apartments to quiet residential streets, Mrs. Frank visibly relaxed. She settled into the seat, and watched the passing scenery. As they neared what Marty now thought of as Will's house, Mr. Frank also relaxed.

"This is exactly the kind of neighborhood we want," he said. "Our children are grown, and we appreciate the kind of place where people take care of their yards. But we also want a place where the grandkids can play outside without some old codger yelling at them to stay out of his flower beds."

Mrs. Frank nodded an emphatic agreement. From her expression, and her husband's tone, Marty was sure they had been in that exact situation, and probably recently.

She smiled as she thought of children running across neatly trimmed lawns. She imagined calling them for dinner, and having them scamper through the neighbor's front yard. She imagined Will coming home from work in time for supper. Her dream stopped there, with a sickening thud.

There was no more Will in her dreams, she reminded herself. It was a fantasy she had concocted, and there was no reason to think that there was anything more than that to it. She forced her thoughts away from Will, and her dreams of him, and back to the conversation at hand.

The Franks were obviously taken with the neighborhood, and when they pulled up in front of Will's house a minute or two later, they were taken with the house.

There was no van in the driveway, though Marty refused to accept that as proof the house was empty after her disastrous visit with Ralph. But when she unlocked the door, and showed the Franks inside, there was an emptiness she had not felt before.

"There has been some recent remodeling work here," she cautioned the Franks, as she led them down the hall. "I don't know if it is all complete, but let's take a look, shall we?"

She led them into the master bedroom, and stopped in shock, but not at any mess.

The room was beautiful. The sliding doors were in place, the mini-blinds had been hung, and the room had been painted a pale green, with accents of the same dark green as the bathroom fixtures. A new light fixture hung from the center of the room, with simple, clean lines of frosted glass and brass accents, to match the plumbing fixtures.

The bathroom had also been completed since her last visit. She showed off the new fixtures to the Franks, and pointed out the view through the garden window, where the landscaping was taking shape.

Although it was late in the year, Will had added evergreens, and there were touches of color. He had also hung mini-blinds of the same pale green as the ones in the bedroom.

They walked back into the bedroom, and Marty raised the blinds, to show off the new, open feeling of the room. That was when she got the next shock. The patio slab, which had once been a forlorn piece of featureless concrete, had been covered with a simple wooden awning, and circled by redwood benches and planter boxes. The effect created a delightful private outdoor retreat. It was shielded from the rest of the house by the fence that surrounded the garden window of the bathroom.

For Marty, who valued her privacy, the secluded patio

was the crowning touch. She realized, with a sudden, hot jolt of jealousy, that *she* wanted this house, even if it meant being reminded of Will every day for the rest of her life.

Somehow he had managed to make this house into the place of her dreams, and she wanted it with an intensity she didn't know she could feel.

She walked the Franks through the rest of the tour, but her heart wasn't in it. She didn't want to sell them the house, she wanted to keep it for herself.

She didn't care about the sales contest, or whether she was the best salesperson in the office. She didn't care about going to the Caribbean, or the beach, or even to dinner. She wanted to sleep in that bedroom, and drink her morning coffee in the solitude of that little patio.

But by the time they had reached the kitchen, where the cabinets had been refaced, and the walls painted to complement the dining room wallpaper, she could see the Franks smiling and exchanging glances. In the way she had come to recognize between long-married couples, their eyes met conspiratorially, and wordless messages passed between them. Marty knew that they were going to buy the house, that they would be the ones to sleep in her bedroom, and have morning coffee on her patio. Their grandchildren would run through the neighbor's yard on their way to dinner. She had seen that look too often in the past to ignore it.

It meant another sale, more points on the contest, and another commission check. But the disappointment of losing the house was sharp and painful.

She reminded herself that she was a professional. The house was just a house. She would be better off without the constant reminders of Will, even though she didn't think she could ever forget him. She stood in the dining room and pretended not to notice the Franks whispering with growing excitement in the kitchen.

As she waited, she could see Will as she had first seen him—standing at the top of the basement steps, water dripping from his hair and clothes, eyes flashing with anger. She examined the new wallpaper, and felt a pale reminder of the electric jolt she had felt when their hands first touched.

She knew she shouldn't think about him. She should turn off the memories, lock them away deep inside where they couldn't get out and hurt her. Pretend he didn't mean that much, and gloss over the pain next time Lorraine or Dotty or Beth asked her about him. She had done it with Charlie, she should be able to do it with Will.

If she could just do that, maybe she could convince herself that the pain wasn't that great after all. Maybe she could believe it, *he,* was just a passing fancy, and she could get on with her life.

The Franks had stopped whispering, and the sudden quiet interrupted Marty's thoughts. It was time to clinch the deal, time to get them back to the office to make the offer. Time to get it over with.

She pushed her memories aside and walked into the kitchen, where the Franks were standing with their arms around each other's waists, a perfect portrait of domestic contentment. They had found a perfect house, and they knew it.

"What do you think about it, now that you've seen it all?" Marty asked, though the answer was written clearly on their glowing faces.

"It's very nice," said Mr. Frank. The caution in his tone was a cover-up, Marty knew. Clients always tried to play hard-to-get when they found what they wanted. They were always afraid to appear too eager.

"I think it might do," said Mrs. Frank, following her husband's lead and covering her enthusiasm. "What's the asking price again?"

They were hooked. Marty knew it, and she should have been elated at making such an easy sale. She should have been relieved that she had finally found a buyer for the house that had haunted her for so many weeks.

Instead her heart was leaden, and her usual high spirits had taken up residence somewhere near her shoes. She quoted the new listing price, which had been raised recently—probably when Will had completed his work on the house.

She wondered where he had found time to finish the work so quickly. Maybe he had hired some help, though that didn't jibe with what he had told her about enjoying the work. Not that it mattered. It looked like he was through with the house, and she was selling it. Soon, neither of them would come back here, and they would forget each other. He would become an amusing anecdote, a short chapter in her life. But she wouldn't tell anyone what an unhappy ending the story had.

"Would you like to see the basement, and the garage?" she asked, passing through the kitchen to the basement door. How she wished Will would come charging up those stairs, like he had before. She pushed the thought aside, opened the door, and turned on the light. She led the Franks down the stairs, and showed them the furnace and the storage areas. She pointed out that the basement was sealed, so that even with the recent heavy rains there was no problem with dampness. She did her job, and she hated every minute of it, especially when they returned to the kitchen, and trooped out to the garage.

Somehow, she had harbored some secret hope that

Will's motorcycle would be there, that she would find him working in the garage.

Instead, it was empty, and spotless. When they locked it behind them, she saw the Franks exchange another secret, wordless signal. They were ready.

"We like this house, and the neighborhood," Mr. Frank began. "There are a couple things we'd like to discuss first, but I think we would like to make an offer to buy."

His wife nodded. "We'll need inspections, of course, and we'll want to see the permits for the recent construction."

"Got stuck one time with a place where the permits weren't in order, and it took an extra six weeks to close the deal, waiting for the city to clear the construction work," Mr. Frank explained. "We're moving soon, and would prefer to have a place to move right into when we get here, rather than having to find something temporary while we mess around with paperwork."

"I understand," Marty said.

Now that the process was underway, she forced herself to let go of the house, give it up to the Franks, and act like a professional. "Why don't we go back to the office and see what we can figure out? I'm sure that the permits are in order, but we will need to check that with the listing agent."

She locked the house carefully behind them. They climbed into her car, and went back to the office. Ninety minutes and two cups of coffee later, they had settled on the wording of the offer, and were waiting for confirmation from George Lane about the permits for the work on the house. Unfortunately, according to his service he was at the football game, and wouldn't be available until late in the evening.

Marty drove the Franks back to their motel, through the deserted streets of the university district. Soon, the stadium would empty and the streets would be jammed with fans. The Franks wanted to be safely settled before that happened.

Marty took them to her favorite Chinese restaurant, and left them at their door with a bag full of take-out containers, and a promise to bring the completed offer for them to sign as soon as she talked to George.

Driving home, it occurred to Marty that she could get the information she needed from Will. He would have been the one to arrange the permits, she was sure, and he could tell her what she needed to know.

Once she was home, with her coat hung on the coat tree, and her shoes kicked under the sofa, she couldn't bring herself to pick up the phone. She wanted desperately to talk to him, but she didn't want to make the first move. He had made it clear he wasn't interested, and she wouldn't humiliate herself again, no matter how innocent she could make it seem.

She didn't consider her decision over-reacting, she was just being cautious and professional. After all, in any other case she would call the listing agent first.

So why was she hovering over the phone, wishing she had the courage to dial Will's number instead of George's?

Will made a final walk-through of the Bakers' house with his foreman. He had asked Tom along as an extra pair of eyes, to spot anything he might have overlooked.

They inspected each room, Tom carrying his clipboard, and Will with his ever-present notebook, but there wasn't anything for them to write down. The house was finished.

Will had thrown himself into finishing it, wanting to put all that it represented behind him. He had said good-bye to one love here, and had fooled himself that he might have found another. Now it was time to move on, time to "get a life" and find out what that life would bring.

Tom glanced down at the blank sheet on his clipboard, and back up at Will. "This place is clean, Will. I wish my own house looked this good. I can't find anything that needs attention."

Will nodded with satisfaction, sticking his notebook back in his pocket. It was what he had thought, but on this project he couldn't trust his own judgment. There was too much of himself tied up in it to be objective.

"Thanks for taking a look, Tom," he said. "I just needed a second opinion before I get the city inspectors to sign off. It's been a long time since I did any residential." He didn't go into any other details, and Tom knew better than to ask. Will had, he knew, a reputation for being a very private boss.

"You should be good to go," Tom said. He stopped at the front door and looked back through the house. "You going to do any more of these rehabs?"

The question startled Will. Had his enjoyment and investment in the project been that obvious? "I've, uh, been thinking about it. Why do you ask?"

Tom shrugged, looking uncomfortable. "Just listening to you, seemed like you really enjoyed this. The way you used to enjoy some of our first projects."

Will shouldn't have been surprised at his observation. Tom had started with Will early on, as a laborer, and worked his way up. They had worked together for years, and Tom knew him as well as anyone on the crew.

Tom had been with him on some of the earliest jobs, when Will was struggling to get started, and working alongside the crew, swinging a hammer. Now Will was mostly an administrator, and Tom headed some of their most elaborate developments. Will had come to depend on him, and sometimes he forgot the days they had worked side by side.

"Besides," Tom continued, "I know a couple guys on the crew who are interested in getting into their own places. Might be a way to work out some of the labor on the next one, if you're interested."

"I'll keep that in mind. Thanks."

Tom left while Will was still digesting his final comment. It might be possible, he supposed, to set up a rehab division. He had been thinking of doing another house by himself, but he would need some help, no matter what. There might be some way he could bring his crew into the projects, and let them gain some sweat equity.

With Tom's idea echoing in his brain, Will took another walk through the house.

He had gone a little overboard in this house, he knew. He had done the work without regard for expense, something he couldn't continue to do. There were things he would have to do differently, if he wanted to make a house affordable, both for himself and for a buyer. He would have to shop carefully for materials, and cut back on some of the luxuries, like the jetted tub.

Some structural changes could be made, though. They could make the house ready for things like the garden window to be added later. New counters could be laminate instead of tile.

He wanted to call Marty, ask her about other houses he could rebuild. He should find out where the residential market stood, too. Even if Tom was right, there was a finite number of his employees. Setting up a division of Hart, Benton and Parker wouldn't make sense unless there was a bigger market than a handful of employees.

The idea took hold of his imagination, sending a shiver

of anticipation through him. He hadn't been this excited about an idea in a long time.

He pulled up his cell phone's directory and had Marty's number on the screen before he stopped himself. Calling Marty, for whatever reason, was a bad idea. She was involved with someone else, and he couldn't settle for just being friends, so it was better to just stay away.

He had never been a believer in the idea that half a loaf was better than none. Somehow he knew, having Marty as a friend would just remind him of all the things he couldn't have. He would be like a kid standing outside the candy store with empty pockets. Just *seeing* the candy would never be enough.

He wiped the number off the screen and put the phone back in his pocket with a force that strained the pocket seams. He'd have George find him another residential specialist.

Preferably a homely old man.

Chapter 23

When the telephone went off before the alarm clock Sunday morning, Marty knew it couldn't be good news. She didn't do mornings well anyway, and she especially hated being awakened by the telephone on the weekend. She debated rolling over and ignoring it, letting the machine pick up the call, but a glance at the alarm told her she only had about forty-five minutes anyway, and that wasn't long enough to get back to sleep properly.

With a groan, she pulled herself out of bed, and padded to the desk in her nightgown, muttering "I'm coming, I'm coming, but this had better be important."

As she reached for the receiver, the answering machine picked up, and she waited while the message played. At the beep, Beth's voice came through, sounding wide awake and full of life.

I hate morning people, Marty thought. Even Beth.

"Beth, I'm here." Marty interrupted Beth's attempt to leave a message after hearing her give her name. "This had better be important, girl. You know how much I love mornings."

"Of course it's important. For heaven's sake, do you think I have a death wish?" Beth's voice rose an octave, and Marty could imagine her waving crimson fingernails in a gesture that dismissed Marty's protests. "Have you seen this morning's newspaper? Of course you haven't. You can't open your eyes before noon on Sunday, much less comprehend written language." Beth's laugh was quick, but Marty heard an undercurrent of tension.

"No, I haven't seen the paper, a fact you already seemed certain of. So maybe you ought to explain what it is that's in the paper, and why you thought it important enough to wake me up before my alarm did. That's a dangerous habit you're developing." Marty was irritated, and she made no attempt to cover the edge of anger in her voice.

"Hey, take it easy, okay?" Beth backed off the jovial tone, and sincere concern crept into her tone. "There's an article in the Real Estate section you ought to see. It seems your buddy Craig is making some legal waves for Home Masters. If you can believe it, he filed a sexual discrimination suit!"

"I already knew about that. We found out a couple days ago from Jerry. There's nothing to it, and nobody around the office is taking it very seriously. Is that all you woke me up for?"

"Honey, the paper is taking it very seriously. I think you better read the article and then call me back."

"I really don't care what that rag prints. Whatever it is, if they're taking Craig's complaint seriously, they're way off base. But I'll go out and get the paper and read it, if it makes you feel better."

"Go. Read. Then you call me back. I want to know what's *really* going on. Bye." The phone went dead in Marty's ear.

Resigned now to staying up, Marty stumbled to the kitchen and put on a pot of coffee. If she had to read about Craig Sailors, the least she could do was fortify herself with caffeine and toast first.

While the coffee dripped, Marty showered and dressed in a pair of knit stirrup pants and a loose tunic top. It was a comfortable outfit for lounging around the house, but sleek enough for a quick trip to the office to retrieve the paperwork for the Franks. She slipped on a pair of flats and ran out to the paper box at the curb. She would check for George Lane's callback after she had her first cup of coffee.

Settled at the kitchen table with coffee and toast, Marty spread the Sunday paper out and thumbed through to the Real Estate section. She felt virtuous, passing up the comics and the advice columns that were her usual Sunday morning amusements. If it was worth Beth calling her early, she should see what they had written.

There it was, in the middle of the page. A full-color picture of Craig, sitting next to his lawyer in a book-lined office. Must be the attorney's office, she thought sourly. Craig wouldn't own a book without pictures.

The caption identified Craig and his attorney, and mentioned the discrimination suit. The headline over the article read "Local Salesman Battles Sexual Discrimination That Threatens His Livelihood."

Marty rolled her eyes. How could anyone believe such a blatant bid for sympathy? She started reading the body of the article, her cynical amusement turning to disgust and then to anger as she read Craig's distorted version of what had happened in the Home Masters office.

There was no mention of his attempt to bribe Dotty, or of the pattern of minor financial and professional liberties Craig had taken. Instead he was portrayed as the victim. He accused Dotty of coming up with the plan that gave him an unfair advantage. The article portrayed Velma as a bitter, unattractive woman, angry because he spurned her advances, and he claimed Ken was jealous of Craig's "friend-ships" with other women in the office.

Marty wondered what other women he was talking about. She and Lorraine certainly didn't have anything resembling a friendship with Craig, unless you counted the fact that Lorraine hadn't clubbed him for the "accidental" physical contacts that happened regularly. He had dismissed Dotty and Velma, and that left only the high school girl that came in afternoons to do clerical stuff—and since she was under-age Marty didn't believe he could be talking about her.

She couldn't believe he had actually taken this to the newspaper. Nor could she understand why they were taking him seriously. Couldn't they see what kind of a manipula-tive creep he was?

In the final paragraph, it said that a Home Masters rep-resentative, they didn't say who, had "declined to com-ment" while the lawsuit was pending. Marty knew the lawyers had asked them not to talk about it, but it meant that their story, the *truth,* wasn't being told.

She picked up the phone to call Beth back. Beth had lis-tened to her gripe about Craig, and she deserved to hear what Marty knew about this latest development.

Beth agreed with her that Craig was an idiot, but she pointed out that a lot of people chose to believe the first story they heard. By getting his side out to the public first, Craig had painted the firm in a bad light, and garnered at least some initial sympathy as the injured party.

"Did you read the sidebar on page three?" Beth asked.

"No, should I?"

"Oh. Well, yeah, you should. He mentions you, and even talks about that old house you were so taken with. Makes some veiled accusations that you were getting special treatment around the office."

"That son-of-a . . ." Marty felt a flush of anger rising in her cheeks.

"Don't I know it. He's been real careful how he says things, probably because his lawyer was sitting there coaching him. But when this is over, somebody ought to take that creep out and teach him some manners. I suggest we start with a cattle prod, and if that doesn't do the trick we can work our way up to baseball bats." Beth didn't believe in subtlety, and Marty appreciated the relish with which she suggested mayhem as the answer to Craig Sailors.

"Men." Marty uttered the one word as though it were the worst curse she knew.

"Sounds like Craig isn't the only one of them giving you trouble, hon. I haven't really talked to you in a couple weeks, you need to catch me up on what the latest is with you and that guy you were dating."

" 'Were' is the operative word there. Things were fun for a while, but I guess it just wasn't meant to be. Haven't seen him in a while, and I don't expect I will again. The house he was working on is selling—in fact I have got to get going, and get some calls made for the buyers—but once that's over with there won't be any reason to see him again. I doubt that I will even see him when this sells, since it looks like the work on the house is finished."

Beth was silent for a moment. Marty could practically hear the worried frown she knew was on Beth's face. "This doesn't sound like the same woman who was telling me this guy *smelled* right, just a couple weeks ago. Just what in the heck happened between you two?"

"Nothing," Marty said. "Nothing happened. We had a few dates, some laughs, and then nothing. That's all there is to it."

"That is not all there is to it. You were completely gone on that guy, and we both know it. You haven't been that crazy about anyone since you married Charlie." Beth's voice had softened to a tone of deep concern. "Something bad happened, and you're not telling me."

"Beth, it wasn't that big a deal. Really, it wasn't. Things just didn't work out."

But Beth wasn't about to take her at her word, and slowly she wormed the story out of Marty. When she had finally told Beth about Will driving away on Halloween, Marty could feel her eyelids stinging.

She blinked rapidly, fighting back the tears she had promised herself she wouldn't shed. No man would do that to her again, not even Will. But she was losing the battle, and as Beth talked Marty felt two hot, fat tears break loose and run down each side of her face. She closed her eyes and let the tears spill over.

"Hon, are you still there?" Beth had run down, and Marty hadn't answered. Marty swallowed hard, and answered with a grunt.

"Marty, this is really hurting you. You're going to have to do something about it. You can't let it go on like this, you'll make yourself sick."

"No I won't." Marty's answer was emphatic. She never got sick, and she certainly wasn't going to let herself go over a man. She had worked too hard to get where she was to throw it away over anyone.

She forced herself to control her voice, and continued. "It wasn't a lot of fun, but I'll get over it. Besides, there isn't anything I can do about it anyway. In the meantime, I have to make a couple calls. You know, a woman's work is never done—especially if she sells real estate. Besides, there will probably be a flap over that article, and I should find out what's going on at the office."

"Okay. For now. But you call me later today. We need to have dinner in the next few days. I need to know you're really all right."

"You just don't quit, do you? Honestly, Beth, if I wanted a mother I have one in California." Marty forced a laugh. "See you later."

When the connection went, she dialed the office, wondering if anyone would be there this early. To her amazement, Dotty answered the phone on the first ring.

In reply to Marty's question, Dotty explained that she had come in as soon as she had seen the Sunday paper. Jerry had called her and told her to keep her chin up, and to tell anyone who called that the company would not comment on the lawsuit or the article, and any reply would be made through their attorney. He was angry, but he was angry at Craig. The question of whether Dotty would stay on seemed settled. Craig's lawsuit had served to solidify her position as one of the team.

"Oh, and Marty, there are three messages here for you from the service. Two from the Franks, they left a phone number at the Phoenix Inn. And there's one from George Lane, says he'll be in the office between eleven and one today."

Marty glanced at the clock. It was nearly eleven. She'd wait to call the Franks until she had talked to George Lane. She wanted to have the answers to their questions before she called them back.

She found the comics and spread apricot jam on a slice of whole wheat toast. She would pretend, at least for a few minutes, that this was a normal Sunday. For a few minutes she would not think about any of the men that had messed up her life.

At a quarter past eleven, Marty put through a call to George Lane's office. He answered the phone himself, to Marty's surprise.

"We don't usually get many calls on Sunday, not like you do at your office. I figured it was either you calling back, or Will calling to cancel our golf game for this afternoon. He was pleased, by the way, that you had a good offer on the house. Said he knew you'd sell it eventually."

The mention of Will's name had Marty's heart racing in her chest. She hadn't even talked to him since that disastrous Halloween dinner, and she wanted desperately to know how he was.

"Glad to hear it." Her voice sounded weak and hollow to her. She hoped George didn't notice. "This couple is very happy with the work that's been done, and they are anxious to know about the permits for the work. Said they'd been caught in a similar situation, where the permits weren't in order, and they didn't want to repeat the experience."

"I haven't been able to reach Will since you called last night. I have seen the permits for most of the work, and I can assure you they are in order, but there was some minor plumbing work that hadn't been signed off on the last time I checked. You could try calling Will directly, if you like, to check on that. Or I could get back to you after I see him this afternoon."

Panic coursed through Marty. How could she possibly call Will for anything? Even if she called about the plumbing work, he was sure to think she had more than pipes and permits on her mind. It would be true, but she certainly didn't want *him* to know that.

No, there was no way she could call him.

"This afternoon will be fine, George. I'll get back to my people, and let them know that most of the work has already been inspected and signed off, and that you are checking on the last of the plumbing inspections. That should be enough to make them happy."

They talked a moment longer, Marty wishing she could ask him about Will, but she was unable to admit to anyone that she cared as much as she did. As long as she refused to admit it, it couldn't be true.

When they hung up, she felt tears stinging her eyes again. She had sworn she wouldn't cry over a man, but that wasn't all that was bothering her. She had held out some hope that the deal with the Franks would fall through, and she would be free to make an offer on the house herself. George's call had dashed that hope. With a heavy heart, she picked up the phone and dialed the Phoenix Inn. Might as well give the Franks their good news.

Will could tell George had something on his mind when he arrived at the country club. There was no sense in asking what; George would speak up when he was ready. Given their last few conversations, Will was happy to wait forever, if it meant he didn't have to be reminded of Karen, and grilled about Marty.

By the back nine, though, he knew George was getting ready to speak up about something.

Will tried to distract him by telling him about the idea of a rehab division. "I've been thinking about doing another house," he said, "and Tom said something the other day that got me to thinking."

Will paused while George putted, then resumed. "He told me some of the guys on the crew were interested in what I did with the Bakers', and might be interested in working on the next project in return for an opportunity to buy the house.

"Seems to me there's got to be a market for something like that. Somewhere between Habitat for Humanity and the regular residential market. We could do a couple houses at a profit, then do one for a guy on the crew, sort of like a co-op."

Will hit his drive, and watched the ball sail down the fairway. His game was on target today, it was George who was distracted.

"What do you think?" he asked after George hooked his drive into the rough. "Think there's a market there?"

George took a deep breath, and turned to look Will in the eye. "There's someone who knows that answer a helluva lot better than I do, Will." He shook his head, disgust evident in his expression and his posture. "It feels like junior high, carrying messages back and forth. Why in the hell don't you just talk to her?"

Will shrugged elaborately, and pretended to concentrate on his chip to the green. "Nothing to talk about," he replied. He drew back the club, knowing the gesture would stifle George's response at least until he completed his shot.

George waited, but the minute Will's club came up he spoke again.

"Bullshit!"

"Now, George! You know the club rules against swearing on the course."

"Don't try to change the subject, Will." George blasted a shot out of the rough, hitting the ball with such ferocity that it sailed over the green. He grimaced as the ball rolled down the far side of the green and stopped on the edge of a sand trap.

"She calls me with questions she would have taken to you directly a couple weeks ago. You call me back, instead of calling her office. It's like junior high," he repeated, "and

I didn't know either one of you then—and I am beginning to feel really glad I didn't!"

Will wouldn't budge. "We don't have anything to say to each other, and I guess she wants to keep it that way. She could have called, and she didn't. I'm just following her lead. You know," he added, a touch of anger creeping into his voice, "moving on."

"Okay, maybe I had that coming," George conceded. He had finally reached the green, and silence descended as he lined up his putt and dropped the ball into the hole.

He continued as he picked up his ball and marked his score card. "Be that as it may, this sure went south fast." The frustration in his voice eased. "But what in the hell happened?"

Will knew he wasn't going to get out of this without giving George some kind of answer. They had been friends a long time, and George would press until he got an explanation.

"There's somebody else. Okay, you happy now?" Will stomped toward the next tee, leaving George to follow along behind.

Panting, George caught up with him. "Slow down, buddy. This isn't a race. And it isn't me you're mad at."

Will shook his head. "Naw. But I got caught up in the idea that she might be special, and I'm out of practice on the whole dating thing."

"No kidding."

Will could hear a note of amusement in his friend's voice. "There's nothing funny about this."

"No?"

"Nothing."

"Listen to yourself. You do sound like somebody in junior high. 'I don't know how to talk to girls.' For heaven's sake, Will, grow up!"

They teed off, and walked down the fairway to where their shots had landed. George's drive was much better, now that he had finally said what was on his mind.

"Okay, okay." Will lined up his shot, gauging the distance to the pin. "You won't have to carry messages any more. I'll get that plumbing permit to you, and that'll take care of it.

"Now, can we just concentrate on the game?"

Chapter 24

"I'm sorry, Ms. Francis, but we have changed our minds about the house. We gave it a great deal of thought this morning, and decided we did not want to make an offer at this time." Mr. Frank's voice was cool and formal, far different from the friendly man she had dropped off with take-out Chinese food the night before.

"Is there a problem?" Marty controlled her voice, but she could feel a sense of foreboding creeping through her. These people had been in love with that house yesterday afternoon. What had happened since then to change their minds?

"Well, Ms. Francis—Marty—my wife keeps telling me that we should just drop the whole thing, but I feel like we owe you some explanation." Marty could hear Mrs. Frank in the background, and although she couldn't make out the words, it was clear that the couple did not agree about how they should proceed.

Mr. Frank whispered something to his wife, the sound muffled as though he held his hand over the receiver. Then he continued talking to Marty, his voice a combination of apology and defiance.

"We thought we were dealing with a reputable firm, and you seemed like a responsible person. But the article in the morning's paper tells a much different story.

"Now, you may be perfectly fine, but it looks like there is a problem, and we don't want to get caught in the middle of it. Whatever is going on, we're just afraid that it could cause some problems for us.

"I'm sorry that we took up your time yesterday, but we didn't know about this problem then, and we just aren't comfortable making an offer under these circumstances. I'm sure you can understand that." Mr. Frank stopped, sounding a little out of breath, as though he had just finished reciting a speech.

Marty counted quickly to ten, letting the silence work on Mr. Frank. She considered and rapidly rejected a number of replies. She could simply shout her anger at the unfairness of such a stance, or cynically ask if they believed everything they read in the newspaper. But none of them would help the situation, and Marty struggled to retain her professionalism.

"I'm terribly sorry that you feel that way. We *are* a reputable firm, and I *am* a responsible person. However, my boss has asked us to refrain from commenting on the lawsuit, and asked that we allow the lawyers to handle all responses." She took a deep breath and continued, determined to salvage as much of the situation as she could. "In any case, I can understand your reluctance to pursue that particular house. However, I do have a couple of similar properties, and I'd be glad to show them to you."

"I'm sorry, Ms. Francis." Marty realized he had gone back to addressing her by her last name. She knew she could kiss this deal good-bye. "We just don't feel that we want to get involved in any way while there is the possibility of any legal complication. I hope you will see our position."

"Certainly, sir." A touch of sarcasm broke through

Marty's carefully controlled professional veneer. "I appreciate your letting me know before I spent any *more* time researching the property for you." She hung up the phone quickly, aware that she was very close to losing her temper with a client.

An ex-client, she reminded herself, thanks to Craig and that shyster of his.

She was shaking, her hands trembling as she held the receiver in its cradle. She couldn't be sure what had upset her more: Craig's arrogance in filing the suit and then taking it to the papers, or the sanctimonious tone Mr. Frank had taken in telling her they were withdrawing from the agreement of the previous evening.

She would call Beth back, and take her up on her offer of dinner. Beth was the one person she could trust herself to talk to when she was this upset, the one person she would allow to see her anger, and her hurt.

When Beth answered the phone, Marty rushed ahead. "Does the dinner offer still stand? Cause if it does, I'll be there about six. And I'll bring the wine."

Beth cooked an early dinner for them at her condo, and they sat talking late into the evening. Marty vented her anger at the loss of the sale, and with it another boost toward the Caribbean cruise.

"You know, Beth, if I win that cruise, you're going to have to go with me. After this," she waved her coffee mug at the clutter of dishes on the table, a gesture that somehow encompassed the emotional conversation of the last couple hours, "you've earned it."

"Don't be silly. You're going to take that guy—Will, right?—with you. Don't tell me that you can't, that you don't want anything to do with him. You can't just shut him out of your life, not after the way you feel."

"And how is it I feel? The guy takes me out a few times, I start thinking maybe it's time for someone new in my life, and then he walks out without even listening to what I have to say.

"I don't even know why. Maybe he saw something, or heard something. If he did, he completely misunderstood it and he's the one making things up.

"Or maybe he just wasn't as interested as I thought he was, and I'm making things up. I have a history of mistaking mild attachments for lifetime commitments, y'know."

"Oh, lighten up! Cynicism doesn't become you, Marty. So you made a mistake with Charlie; that doesn't have to scar you for life. Besides, he was the one who proposed, so he thought it was a lifetime commitment, too. He was the one who couldn't make a long-term relationship work. God knows, *you* tried.

"But whatever happened with *this* guy, you need to find out. If you can't fix it, at least get the facts and learn from it."

Marty shrugged. She wanted to call Will, to make him listen. But she didn't know how to talk to him, to find out what he wanted from her.

As she relaxed, Marty began to realize that there might be a silver lining to this cloud, after all. If the Franks had withdrawn their offer to buy the house, she could buy it herself. She wouldn't get credit for the contest, but she could have her dream house.

The thought made her relax, and she felt the corners of her mouth turning up in a ghost of a smile. Beth could see the lightening of her mood, and looked at her quizzically.

"I just realized, Beth. With the Franks withdrawing, I can buy the house!"

"You want that place? Why? It'll make you think of him every day."

"Maybe. But it's exactly what I want. All the work that's been done, was done for me. It's how I would have done it. In fact, it's how I *told* him to do it. He wanted my suggestions, and he acted on every one of them.

"That house was made for me, and I intend to have it." Marty knew she could call her banker in the morning, and start the financing process. With luck, she would be in the house in time for the holidays. Well, maybe not Thanksgiving, but definitely before Christmas.

By the time Marty left Beth and headed home, she was convinced that it had all been for the best. With the Franks out of the picture, the dream house was hers.

She would live in it by herself, and enjoy the solitude. She would buy wrought iron furniture for the deck off the master bedroom, and thick, fluffy white towels for the new bathroom. She imagined the bedroom with a brass bed, and sleek oak furniture. It would be the home she had always wanted.

And who cared whether there were children running through the neighbor's flower beds, anyway?

When she got her banker on the phone late the next morning, however, Craig's lawsuit had already done its damage.

"I'm sorry, Marty," Tim said in a low voice. "Right now would not be a good time for you to be applying for any new loans. I really shouldn't even be talking to you about this, and I certainly wouldn't be, if we were talking about an actual application. But as long as this is simply a casual conversation between a couple of friends, about a hypothetical loan, I'd advise you to wait a little while and see if Jerry can get this thing settled before you make any financial commitments.

"Don't get me wrong, nobody is worried about your existing mortgage, or your line of credit, or anything. It's just that, in light of this lawsuit, Home Masters isn't exactly a strong employer. If this guy prevails, he could own the place, and you know how long your job would last. Even if he doesn't, the negative publicity is going to hurt you."

Tim resumed a more normal tone. "Do you remember what happened to Systemco? They didn't do anything wrong, the court upheld them, but they lost almost seventy percent of their business in the year that dragged on."

Marty remembered all too well. She had had friends who lost jobs and homes when Systemco finally filed bankruptcy.

Marty's stomach felt hollow. Craig had robbed her of a sale, ruined her relationship with a potential client, and now his blasted lawsuit was destroying her plans to buy her dream house.

She thanked Tim, and quietly hung up the phone. Between Will's disappearance and Craig's lawsuit, how much worse could her life get?

The phone rang, as though in answer to her question, and she jumped. What kind of bad news would this be?

She had to stop wallowing in self-pity, and get back to work. If she just worked a little harder, she could find a way out of this mess.

She took a deep breath, and answered the phone.

Ralph's voice boomed at her from the other end of the line. "Hey, darlin', what gives with that jerk who filed this lawsuit? I can't believe he thinks he can get away with it, and especially with bad-mouthing you like that."

"Thank you, Ralph." Marty found herself smiling at the indignation in Ralph's voice. He was a true friend. "I appreciate the vote of confidence, but 'that jerk' as you so sweetly called him, has managed to upset a lot of people."

"Let me tell you something, girl." Ralph's voice was quiet and serious. "I knew that guy was a real creep from the get-go. A few months back I had a run-in with him, one day when you were out. I didn't say anything about it, since he steered clear of me after that, but now it sounds like something you ought to know."

Marty's heart raced, and her throat suddenly went dry. She swallowed hard, afraid to ask for details. Afraid what Ralph knew wouldn't be enough.

Finally she managed to force the words out. "A run-in? What happened?"

Ralph, in his brusque, businesslike way, explained that Craig had told him Marty was unavailable, and that he, Craig, would be taking over some of her clients. He insisted that Ralph should talk to him, and Marty would be out for an extended period.

As he talked, Marty pulled her date book from her battered briefcase, and checked her calendar for the past few months.

She hadn't been out of the office much over the summer. The only possible time was when she had been off work for three days with a root canal, early in June. Ralph confirmed the time, and detailed Craig's lies.

"Ralph, would you repeat this to Jerry and Ken? They need to know what you've told me. I think it could be very important in defending us against this suit."

"Sure, darlin'. That's why I brought it up. I'll be glad to talk to them. But that wasn't the only reason I called."

"What can I do for you? Just name it."

Marty's hand was shaking so badly from the adrenaline rush, she had to clutch the receiver tightly against her ear to keep from dropping it. "If the stuff you told me is as important as I think it is, your wish is my command."

"That's a tempting offer, but for now I think I'd settle for another look at that house out on Agate. I keep thinking about that place, and wondering how the work came out." Ralph sounded suddenly shy, almost sheepish. "I need to take another look, a real close one."

Marty knew when Ralph took a "real close" look at a place, it usually ended with lots of paperwork and big checks. She hated to let go of the house, but the conversation with the banker came back to her. On the other hand, if Ralph could provide the ammunition, maybe Jerry *could* get it settled, and then she could get her loan. On the other hand, if he gave them the key to getting Craig off their backs, she would owe him a great deal. She had to play it straight with Ralph, her conscience wouldn't allow her not to.

If she had to sell the house to someone else, if she couldn't buy it herself, she couldn't think of anyone better than Ralph. He had seen the same potential she had, and he would appreciate it as much as she would.

Her voice dragged with reluctance, but she had to ask. "You're going to buy it, aren't you?"

"I do believe I am. If the work's done right. But you ought to be pleased. You dragged me out there, knowing I wouldn't be able to forget the place once I'd seen it. And you were right.

"Now, when can we go take a look?"

Chapter 25

Marty glanced at Jerry's office, again. Ralph was still shut in the office with Jerry, Ken, and Velma. She knew Jerry's lawyer had been called, and had called back a short while later—thanks to Dotty's willingness to keep her posted.

The four of them had been talking for what seemed like a very long time, though she knew it had really only been about an hour. She had promised to take Ralph out to look at the house when they were finished, but she was about ready to give up and go get a burger.

The door opened, and Jerry emerged, the ghost of a smile playing across his face. He motioned for Marty to join them in the office.

"Martha," Jerry never used nicknames, "I wanted to thank you for bringing Mr. Gordon to talk to us. I know you two had an appointment this afternoon, and I don't want to hold you up any longer."

Marty nodded. She wanted to pepper them all with questions, to find out what was going on, and maybe get some reassurance that life would get better. But she held her tongue. Jerry would tell her when he was ready, and no amount of questioning would shake a word loose until then.

"I would appreciate if you would keep this quiet for now, however. We have talked with our lawyer, and he is in the process of contacting Mr. Sailor's attorney. With the information that Mr. Gordon has given him, we are confident we can reach a quick, and painless, conclusion to this whole episode."

Marty nodded again. If it was good news, they would all know soon enough. And if it wasn't, there was no sense in getting everyone's hopes up for no reason. Still, in her heart, she knew Ralph had solved the problem of Craig Sailors. The air in the room seemed lighter somehow, and Jerry couldn't suppress a smile.

"Thank you for your cooperation. We may need Mr. Gordon back here this afternoon. Our lawyer seemed to think he might need to sign an affidavit or something. But in the meantime, why don't you go ahead and take care of your business?"

Ralph stood up, and shook hands with Jerry, then Ken and Velma. The relief on all three faces was plain, in contrast with the strain that had been there earlier in the day. Marty and Ralph walked out to her car, and drove south.

"Ralph, you're a lifesaver. I don't know how much damage that suit could have done, but I do have to tell you, it already cost me one sale."

"You're kidding! I can't believe anyone would back out of a deal just because of the stuff that guy told the newspaper."

"Oh, believe it. I had a couple that were ready to buy this house on Saturday, but before I could get the answers to a couple questions, they saw that article and dropped it like a hot potato. And not just this place, they gave me the bum's rush like I've never seen it."

Marty parked in front of the house. It looked lonely, with the bare November rose bushes. The drapes were drawn in the living room, and there was a deserted air about the place. Marty realized this was the first time she had come there knowing Will wouldn't be there. Without that possibility, it seemed even darker and more forlorn.

Walking through the living room, and down the hall, they could see that the work was, indeed, finished. There were no signs of anyone. No tools left behind in anticipation of returning to complete a job. No blinds waiting to be hung, or light fixtures to be installed.

The house was complete, and it was perfect.

They explored the rooms, and Ralph expressed continuing approval of the choices Will had made.

Marty was reminded again and again that this was the way she had envisioned it when Will first asked her for her suggestions. This was the house as she had dreamed it, and Will had brought that dream to life. Now she had lost Will, and she was about to lose the house, too.

She stood in the kitchen, leaning one hip against a counter, as Ralph explored the basement. She listened to his tread on the stairs as he came back up. It reminded her of her first visit, and she watched Ralph come through the door where she had first seen Will.

Maybe Beth was right, maybe this wasn't a good place for her to be. But it was the house she had dreamed of, and she still wanted it.

"It's right." Ralph brushed his hands together, wiping away a few traces of imaginary dust from the basement. "I want it, and I'm willing to pay top dollar. Just get me the paperwork, and I'll put my name on the dotted line. No need for any contingencies, I've already spoken with my accountant and the money will be available immediately."

"You knew you were going to buy it before you came out here." It wasn't a question, but a statement.

"Yes, I did. But I needed to see you in the house again. I

had to be sure this was the right place."

"Right for what?"

Ralph crossed the room, and put his hands on her waist. With a strength Marty didn't know he had, he lifted her easily onto the counter, and sat her down.

"I think you need to just sit and listen to what I have to say, darlin'." He kept his hands resting loosely on her waist. She waited, sitting very still. Ralph's eyes were dark and solemn, so unlike the jocular fellow that had been her friend over the years.

"This house belongs to you, Marty. You made it. It doesn't matter who did the work, or what suggestions anyone else made. You made this house with your dream of it. I don't quite know how you saw it, but you did, and it's just the way I would have wanted it, too.

"We're a lot alike, you and me. Our tastes are similar, we laugh at a lot of the same things, and we're both dedicated to our jobs. I think we'd make a good team."

Marty looked cautiously at him. She wasn't sure exactly what she was hearing, but she didn't want to interrupt. Ralph was no longer talking in his businesslike to-the-point manner. This was personal, and if she gave him time, he would explain himself. He just had to take a roundabout route sometimes.

"What I'm trying to say, darlin', is that I want you to marry me."

Time stood still. Marty had longed to hear those words, but not from Ralph. She cared for him a great deal, but she wasn't in love with him, and she couldn't possibly marry him. But how could she tell him that without hurting him?

"I, um, I'm, uh, well, I'm really flattered," she stammered. "But I had no idea you felt this way." She took his hands from her waist, and held them in hers. She looked in

Ralph's eyes, wishing they were Will's gray ones.

"It wouldn't work, Ralph. Sure, we're a lot alike, and we have similar tastes. You would respect my work, and I would respect yours. We would make a fine team in many ways, and we enjoy each other's company." She held Ralph's eyes with hers, and took a deep breath.

"But there's one thing that you didn't mention."

Something shifted in Ralph's gaze. For an instant, Marty could see a depth of pain she had never known existed. "What is that, Marty? Is it love? You know we both tried that before, and we both know it didn't work. We're compatible, and I'm willing to settle for that. I just want a little comfort and companionship in my old age."

Anger flooded Marty's body. She gripped Ralph's hands tighter, and glared at him. "You aren't that old, dammit!" Ralph flinched at the unexpected anger. He had never heard Marty swear before. "And you shouldn't 'settle' for anything! Just because you had one relationship go sour on you doesn't mean you can't find another one, if you just stop hiding behind all that bluff and bluster. I care a great deal about you, Ralph Gordon, and that's one reason why there is no way I'm going to marry you. You deserve more than what you and I have together, and I won't spoil a perfectly good friendship by trying to pretend it's enough to build a marriage on."

Marty pushed him away, intending to hop off the counter and storm out of the room. She couldn't let Ralph sell himself short this way. It wasn't right. But Ralph caught her in his arms as she slid off the counter, and held her close.

She pushed him away, but he held onto her, and looked deeply in her eyes. In his eyes, she saw the pain break away, and a wave of relief wash over him. "You really believe that, don't you? You really believe love is possible the second time around."

She nodded, looking away. There was something disturbingly familiar about what he was saying, but she couldn't place it.

"And you think I can find it?" Ralph continued. "I'm not so sure about that. But you are." He tilted her chin up, forcing her to look at him again. "That's because you've found it, haven't you, Marty? It's because you're in love, just not with me. You won't settle for companionship, because you know something more is possible."

Marty knew what Ralph was saying was true. She was in love, and she had been for weeks. She just didn't want to admit it, to let herself be vulnerable, to let herself be hurt. She nodded her head, and Ralph's grip loosened.

"Is it the guy who was fixing up this house? Is that the lucky guy who's beating my time?"

Marty frowned, feeling the anxiety etching lines across her brow. Ralph was smiling, waiting for her to admit what he had already guessed. She didn't need to say anything, she knew Ralph could see it in her eyes.

"It is him," he said. "He's a lucky man. Now, my dear friend, I want you to tell me all about him. And he had better be worth you loving him."

Ralph released her, but slipped one arm protectively around her shoulders. "You can fill me in on the way back to the office. I'm still buying this house."

Marty talked to Ralph while they drove slowly back to the office. She told him about Will, about the way he made her feel. Finally, as she parked the car in the lot, she turned to him.

"There's something else you need to know. I don't think anything will ever come of this. I don't think he's as interested in me as I am in him."

"If he isn't, he's a fool. And this Will of yours doesn't sound like a fool to me. What makes you think so?"

She told him the story of the Halloween dinner, and her attempt to explain her friendship with Ralph. "But he didn't want to listen. He just said that he assumed I had other friends, and I didn't owe him any explanations, and he left. I just don't think he cared enough to let me explain."

"There may be another reason, darlin'. If he thought there was something between us, he might have been gentleman enough to bow out without making a scene. He may have been trying to give you a graceful way out of something you didn't want to be in."

Marty pounded her fist on the steering wheel. "Then why didn't he say so? Why didn't he find out if I wanted a way out? No, he just drove off, and left me standing there, feeling like a prize fool."

Ralph reached over and took her hand. "Don't be too hard on him. He may not have been any more sure than you were. Men aren't immune, you know. We can be prize fools, too."

Marty winced. Could Will be hiding his true feelings?

She didn't want to consider the possibility that she had been so wrong. It would mean she had thrown away a chance at true love. "In any case, it doesn't matter. He hasn't even called me, and I haven't seen any sign of him around the house in the last week or so. In fact, I think he hired out the last of the work on the house, and got it all done so he wouldn't have to go over there any more."

Ralph shrugged. "Maybe. Or maybe there's another reason. But you'll never know if you don't talk to him."

"We'll see." Marty dismissed the subject. Ralph was a

dear friend, and always would be, but he was starting to sound an awful lot like Beth.

Beth. That was what was so familiar about her talk with Ralph. She had been telling him the same things Beth had been telling her, but she had refused to believe. So maybe Beth had been right. But how would she ever know?

"There is one other thing." Marty's voice was brisk, dismissing the intimate tone that had surrounded the pair for the past hour. "That briefcase you gave me. It's still sitting in the office, still in the wrapping from the luggage store. I want you to take it back. I'm really afraid that I took it under false pretenses, now."

Ralph matched her tone, all business again. "I won't take it back. There is no way I am going to let you return that gift. I gave it to you because you're a friend, and you have given me a great deal of help and special service over the years. It's a business gift, a way of thanking you for your help, and a gift of friendship. There were no strings attached when I gave it to you, and there are none now. Please don't think any of that has changed."

Marty and Ralph walked into the office, and were met at the door by Dotty. "Jerry's been asking for you. He had to go out, but he said for you to page him the minute you got back. He seemed very pleased about something, Marty, and I have a hunch it has to do with your friend here." She grinned up at Ralph, who grinned in return.

"Can you do that for us? This lady here has to sell me a house." Dotty nodded to Ralph, and hurried back to her desk.

Ralph followed Marty to her desk, where he slouched in the visitor's chair and waited while she started writing up the paperwork. Halfway through the earnest money agreement, Ralph interrupted her and asked to use her phone.

She pushed the instrument toward him, not taking her eyes from the documents in front of her.

As she wrote, Marty could hear Ralph talking on the phone, and she realized he must be speaking to his accountant. By the time she had the offer written, Ralph had hung up with a satisfied smile on his face.

"He says the money will be in the bank on Wednesday. If this goes quickly, I could be moved in time to watch the Thanksgiving football games in my new house."

"Don't hold your breath, Ralph. I don't see any way this deal can be done in less than two weeks. And the offer hasn't been accepted yet. You look over this," she pushed the completed agreement across the desk, "while I call George and ask him to present it to his sellers."

"Go ahead and call, but I don't see why you don't just call the man and present the offer yourself." Ralph's tone was casual, but Marty was chilled by the prospect. She just wanted to get this over with, and be rid of the humiliating possibility that she might have to see Will again.

She talked with George Lane, and he arranged to take the offer to Will immediately. "He should be home from the capital by now," he said. "I'll call him, then spin by and pick up the paperwork. It sounds like an excellent offer, and my advice will be for him to accept it immediately."

"The capital?" Marty echoed, feeling vaguely uneasy.

"Sorry, I shouldn't have mentioned it." George gave a small, embarrassed laugh. "He's testifying before the State Senate on a new development bill. He hates for people to know, but he's the Hart of Hart, Benton and Parker."

Marty recognized the name immediately. It was the most successful real estate developer in the area. Their name was featured prominently in the business section nearly every day, in connection with transactions of all sorts. She had read about Will's prowess with Pacific Rim developments on many occasions, but his picture had never been attached to the articles, and she hadn't made the connection. Until now. It certainly explained how he could spend the kind of money he had put into the Agate house, to benefit his absent friends.

"I see. Well, there was no reason I had to know of course, but I appreciate you explaining it to me. The papers will be ready for you to pick up any time today." She looked up at the wall clock. It was already after four. "I'll be around the office for a while yet, or you can call me at home if this isn't taken care of until late."

She promised to leave the paperwork at the reception desk for him if she left before he got there, and hung up. Ralph was looking at her, one eyebrow cocked in question.

She tried to ignore the unasked question, and examined the document Ralph had signed. He gave an exasperated sigh, and pulled the paper out of her hands.

"It hasn't changed since you wrote it five minutes ago. All I did was sign it. Now stop stalling, and just tell me what the guy said."

"He'll be by to pick up the papers in a few minutes, and he'll take them over to the sellers' representative. If he accepts your offer, we'll have a deal." She pulled the paper back, and busied herself separating the carbonless copies and placing one set in an envelope.

Ralph reached back across the desk, and grabbed her hands in his. "There was something else. Something that has you distracted. Was it something about the deal?"

"No, Ralph. The deal will be fine. You'll have the house, I'm sure of it. George told me he would advise his sellers to accept the offer immediately. There won't be any problem."

"Then what is it?" Ralph's face was clearly worried.

"You aren't the type to fidget, but you're practically vibrating, you're so tense. What was it he said, something about the capital?"

Marty sighed. Ralph was persistent, and she knew she couldn't avoid giving him an answer. "All right, but don't tell anyone, okay? It seems that my handyman has a couple other things to fill his days. You know the name Hart, Benton and Parker?" Ralph nodded. Anyone who did business in town knew the name. "Well, Will's last name is Hart—as in William B. Hart, of Hart, Benton and Parker. I feel like a complete jerk for not making the connection."

"So. You're in love with one of the richest guys in the county. You could have done a lot worse. And from what I remember of him—we met a couple years ago at some university dinner—he's not bad-looking, either. So what next?"

"So nothing, Ralph. We let George take your offer to his client, and then we buy you a house. Then we're done, and we all go our separate ways, and I try to forget him."

"We'll see." Ralph shrugged, and rose from his chair. Dotty signaled him to pick up the phone. He spoke for a couple minutes, then hung up. "I've got some things to do, and your boss wants me to stop by his lawyer's office right now. Just leave a message on my machine to let me know if he accepts. Then we'll take it from there. But you better think about what you want, darlin'. If you truly believe we get a second chance at love, you'd be a fool to let it get away."

Left alone at her desk, Marty tried to make sense of the last few weeks. She was in love with Will, she had admitted that to herself, and to Ralph. But what was she going to do about it?

Nothing. She was going to do nothing about Will. In fact, there was nothing she could do. She was going to put her life back together, get the Agate house sold so she could forget about it, and concentrate on winning the sales contest.

Especially the sales contest. Craig had turned it into a personal struggle between them, and had continued the conflict through the lawsuit. She was determined to beat him.

Lorraine sailed through, and stopped for a brief, one-sided conversation. "Wish me luck. I'm going out to show a house down in that same neighborhood south of the university. Been a little hotbed of activity out there this fall, hasn't it?" She waved a hand at Marty, and bustled toward the door.

Marty sighed. The office was quiet after Ralph and Lorraine had left, and she couldn't concentrate on the papers on her desk. But she was afraid to leave, afraid she would miss George's call accepting Ralph's offer. She wanted the house sold, to put an end to this chapter of her life. She just wanted it all to be over.

She had to keep busy. Reaching under the credenza, she pulled out the box from the luggage store, and carefully unwrapped the briefcase. It was beautiful, and she knew Ralph had spent far too much on it, but she had agreed to keep it. It would remind her every day of the value of friendship. She slipped the gift card into her desk drawer, and stuffed the wrappings in her wastebasket. It was time for a change.

Propping the lid open, she set the two briefcases side-by-side on the credenza, and began to carefully transfer the contents of one to the other.

Chapter 26

The phone rang as Marty finished cleaning out her old briefcase, and sliding it back under the credenza. She wasn't sure she was ready to throw it away, but she wouldn't be using it any more.

Marty looked up, and realized that the office had emptied while she was occupied with her task. She answered the phone, which had continued to ring. It was George.

"The deal looks fine to us. Thanks for finding us this guy. You did us all a great favor, and we appreciate it. Now I remember why I got out of residential property." He chuckled. "Will agreed to it immediately, but we had to wait until he could call his friends and get their approval. He does have a power of attorney, and the signed contracts will be on your desk tomorrow."

"That's good news, George. I'll let my buyer know that the deal is set. He wants to get this through as quickly as we can, so he can move. He's never been big on patience, once he's made up his mind on something."

"Shouldn't be any problem on this end. Just let me know if there's anything else you need from us. And thanks again." George hung up, and Marty dialed Ralph's number. She got his answering machine, and left her home number.

Transferring the phones to the service, Marty locked up

the office, and walked across the darkened parking lot to her car. Ten minutes later, as she walked through her front door, she heard the answering machine click off.

She listened to the recording of the call she had just missed. It was Ralph, returning her call. She shook her head in amazement. How did people conduct their lives before answering machines? It seemed impossible to actually talk to anyone without first talking to their machine two or three times.

She called him back and gave him the good news. Finally, the Agate house was out of her life. Some formalities, a pile of paperwork, and she would never have to think about it, or Will, again.

Will signed the last of the papers and handed them back to George Lane. "Thanks for the help."

George nodded, and put the papers in a file folder for the escrow company.

"One more thing, George."

George looked up, his eyes wary.

Will held up a hand, as if to stop a question he knew was coming. "Nothing to do with her, I swear. I just want you to make a couple calls, find out if there's anybody around doing the kind of rehab stuff I'm thinking about."

"Way ahead of you." George sounded pleased with himself. "After our golf game, I knew you'd be asking, and you wouldn't want to wait." He shook his head. "You never were very good at waiting."

Will laughed. He hadn't laughed in a long time, not since Halloween, and it felt good. "You know me too well. What have you got?"

"I talked to a couple guys I know, and they told me about a local, Ralph somebody, who's been doing this kind of stuff on the side. One of them told me he was getting out, wanted to do something else. Said he'd have Ralph give you a call, if you're interested in talking to him."

"Good idea. If the guy will talk to me, maybe I can find out whether this is worth a new division, or if I should just do it myself when I need a break."

Will stood up and stretched. "Long drive, and I have to do it at least once more this week.

"I'd like to buy this Ralph dinner one night this week. Sweetwater's. Pass the message for him to call Rita, if he's willing to talk. Whatever works for him, I'll be there."

"Sure thing." George waved as Will opened the door. "I'll pass along the invitation."

The maitre d' greeted Will at the entrance to Sweetwater's. Rita had reserved a table for him as soon as she had heard from Ralph, and relayed the information to Will in the capital.

He had driven straight through from Salem in order to make the appointment, and he was feeling a bit dragged out. As he was escorted to the table, he asked the maitre d' to have the busboy bring him a cup of coffee. He would regret the caffeine later, but he needed a boost right now.

As they walked through the restaurant, Will thought he recognized a man sitting alone near the windows overlooking the river. He had only seen him once, but the image of his lips pressed against Marty's forehead was burned into his memory.

With growing horror, he realized he was being led to the man's table. "Ralph something" was Marty's friend, the one he had seen her with in the Bakers' house.

He had been set up!

Rita had sounded a little odd when she passed on the

date for his dinner, but he thought she was just more rushed than usual, with him out of the office. Now he wondered how much she had known. He hadn't even mentioned Marty at the office, as far as he could remember, but Rita had been with him a long time, and she sometimes seemed to guess more than he ever told her.

And George. Some people just never knew how to butt out. He would never believe this was just coincidence. George must have known what he was leading Will into. He was going to have some explaining to do.

Nearby tables were discreetly empty, which meant Rita had told them this was a business meeting, but there were other diners in the restaurant. Will was approaching the table, and there was no graceful way to back out.

Well, he could have his coffee, and then beg off dinner. He would pay for Ralph's dinner, he had issued the invitation after all. But he would stay only as long as was necessary for the sake of appearances.

Anger rose in him. George had been right, this was like junior high. Like the time Brad Bowden took Jennifer Stacy to the spring dance.

But this time they weren't in the schoolyard, and he couldn't take out his frustration by pounding the other guy. Much as he might want to, that was a part of his life he had put behind him. He had other ways of dealing with problems.

Despite his resolve, though, as soon as the maitre d' was out of earshot, he could only manage to say, "You!"

The man stood and held out his hand. "Ralph Gordon."

Will shook his hand briefly, aware they were in a very public place. He quickly released his grip, and sat down heavily.

Ralph smiled pleasantly at him, as though this was a

simple social occasion. Will wanted to swear at him, but he held his tongue. Clearly, Ralph knew who he was, and had planned this evening. Well, he wasn't going to help the guy out.

Will didn't speak, waiting for Ralph to explain himself. As though there was anything the man had to say that he wanted to bother listening to.

Ralph sat looking at him for long minutes. Finally, he leaned forward. "You don't want to talk to me, do you? Can't say as I'd blame you, if the tables were turned."

Ralph glanced around the room, then looked hard at Will. "But you'll have to at least listen for a few minutes. Can't walk out as soon as you walk in."

Will didn't answer. The guy understood the bind he was in, and he was going to have his say. He'd won, and now he had to gloat. He had better be quick about it.

"Shit." Ralph spoke quietly, a grim smile curling his lips. "I want to be madder than hell at you, but we have too much in common."

Will furrowed his brow in an unspoken question, and Ralph grinned. "You have no idea what I'm talking about, do you?"

When Will shook his head, Ralph started to answer, then quickly stopped as the waiter approached with a pair of shrimp cocktails.

"I ordered them," Ralph said after the waiter left. "Figured I might need some food on the table to keep you here."

"Go ahead." They were the first two words Will had spoken since sitting down.

"You've been bitten by the rehab bug, so I hear. It's a great feeling, putting a house back together, and there are plenty of houses around town that need work. So there's the answer to the question you already asked."

Will's stomach growled, reminding him he hadn't eaten since late morning. He picked up his fork and speared a shrimp. He was hungry, they were right there, and he would be paying for them. Might as well eat.

Ralph leaned back a little, settling into his chair. "There are a couple other questions you haven't asked. Maybe you didn't want to ask, maybe you didn't think I'd answer. But I'm happy to help you out."

Ralph picked up his fork and speared a shrimp, before putting it in his mouth, he said, "I've been doing this for a few years as a sideline, and I'm kind of burned out, ready to settle down."

Yeah, with a cute little redhead, I'll bet. Will hoped his thoughts weren't as obvious as they felt.

"I asked her," Ralph said, as though Will had actually spoken aloud. He swallowed and looked hard at Will. "Really thought she might take me up on it. She's a great woman. But she turned me down."

Will stopped with another shrimp halfway to his mouth. "Not much for subtlety, are you?"

Ralph laughed, and shook his head. "No, not really. With me, what you see is pretty much what you get.

"I don't like to beat around the bush, Hart. I'm blunt, and I find it makes my life a lot easier. Now, if you want to order some food, I think I can help you out with your little problem."

Late the next morning, Jerry called them all into a meeting in the conference room. He had Dotty route the calls to the service, and Velma appeared with boxes of doughnuts and a wide smile.

"Ladies and gentlemen, when Mr. Sailors hit us with

that lawsuit earlier this month, we promised to keep you informed. Yesterday, one of our clients came forward with some information. We spent some time with my lawyer yesterday afternoon, and I am pleased to announce that we have reached an agreement. This settlement is contingent on some of you agreeing to the terms, but I doubt any of you will object."

He handed a stack of papers to Ken, who passed them around the room. The single sheet listed the major points of the settlement.

"As you can see, Mr. Sailors has withdrawn his allegations. He has asked that we keep the terms under which he withdrew them confidential, and we three have agreed. However, we must ask that the rest of you agree, as well.

"In return, Mr. Sailors has resigned his real estate license in this state, and agreed not to seek another job in real estate. He has signed an agreement relinquishing any claim as regards the sales contest, and offered a letter of apology.

"I realize that this is small compensation for the trouble, loss of business, and damage to our reputation that he caused. His attorney advised him that we were being extremely generous under the circumstances, and told him it was in his best interest to accept our offer. The newspapers will be notified that a settlement has been reached, and will be given a broad outline, though the details will be confidential.

"If you are in agreement, we can put this business behind us. Any questions?"

Marty raised her hand. "The publicity directly cost me a sale. I know I won't get any compensation, and that really isn't that important, but will I be able to show that letter of apology to my clients? I would like to be able to clear my reputation."

"There will be a public version of the letter, which can be shown to clients, if necessary. Any other questions?" He paused. "I do want to say, privately, that I would dearly love to give this jerk what he really deserves. But between my lawyer and Velma, they have convinced me that it would cost us so much in time, money, and bad publicity, that it is best to put it behind us."

Heads nodded around the room. An immense feeling of relief swept through the assembled staff, and soon the gathering took on the feel of an impromptu celebration.

Marty relaxed for the first time in weeks. The crisis had passed, and life could return to normal. Or as normal as her life would ever be.

The next few days passed in a blur of paperwork. Marty was continually surprised at the amount of leverage Ralph seemed to have, and he got things done as fast as he wanted them.

To her delight, the sale of the Agate house, and the settlement of Craig's lawsuit, had put her in first place in the sales contest. She was going to the Caribbean in the spring, after all. With Beth, but she was going.

The day after Ralph's house closed escrow, he called Marty. She was pleased to hear his voice boom out of the phone.

"This place is looking great, darlin'. The movers are here unloading the furniture, and I'll have a devil of a job unpacking it all, but it's going to be great. This house is going to be just right."

"Glad to hear it, Ralph."

"There's just one thing."

"You name it. We all owe you for getting that lawsuit settled so quickly."

"You have to come to Thanksgiving dinner. I don't really care what other plans you thought you had. Cancel them, or bring them along, but you're coming to Thanksgiving in my new house, and I'm not taking no for an answer."

Marty hesitated. She and Beth had a standing date for Thanksgiving. They went to dinner at Sweetwater's, and spent the evening seeing movies. The theaters were nearly empty on Thanksgiving night, and they sometimes saw two or three pictures. But she owed Ralph a great deal.

"We'll be there. I have a date with my best girlfriend, but if I can bring her along . . ."

"Of course. You know I never turn down a chance to spend time with a beautiful woman."

"How do you know she's beautiful?" Marty laughed. Ralph's good spirits were infectious.

"How could she not be? All women are beautiful in one way or another. I just need to open my eyes. Someone reminded me recently that we all need to open up and let the possibilities happen."

There was a note of glee in Ralph's voice that made Marty wonder just what he was up to, but she remembered the other housewarming parties he had thrown when he moved. He was always excited when he moved into a new house.

"What time?" she asked.

"Let's have dinner about three. And don't worry about the food. I'm not cooking, the caterers will bring it all, and we just have to sit down and enjoy. We'll see you then." He hung up before she could ask any more questions—like who "we" meant.

When Marty reached Beth at home that evening, she
agreed to the change in plans. "Why not do something a
little different this year? I'd love to see this house anyway,
since I never did get over and check it out while it was on
the market. I must admit I'm curious about it. I mean, I
heard about it every time I talked to you in the past three
months."

"You did not."

"Marty, you were practically obsessed with that house.
I'm glad it's sold. Now you can stop worrying about it."

Marty had to admit it was true. She had thought nearly
the same thing herself earlier that week. Still, it would seem
strange to see it with Ralph's things all moved in. She wondered how she would feel about it.

Beth picked up Marty on Thanksgiving afternoon. The
day was clear, but cold, and the promise of winter was
strong. Rain had left the ground soft, the trees still held a
few gold and red leaves, though most of them had fallen,
and the evergreens showed blue-green against the surrounding foothills. They drove through town, enjoying the
beauty of the day.

When they arrived at Ralph's new house, there was a
strange pickup in the driveway. Ralph hadn't mentioned
that he'd invited other people, though there was no reason
he should have told her. She remembered the "we" in his
invitation, and wondered idly who else might be there.
They found a parking place on the street, and hurried up
the front walk. There was a sharp wind that put a lie to the
bright sunshine of the afternoon.

Marty rang the bell, and waited for Ralph to answer the
door. She had turned away slightly, looking over the neighbor's lawn, when she heard the door open. Turning back,

she opened her mouth to greet her host.

Whatever words had been forming in her head never made it to her lips. She stood frozen, staring into the soft gray eyes of Will Hart. He held the door open, and reached for her hand.

"Won't you please come in?"

Marty stood still, unable to move. What was he doing here? He didn't belong here any more; it was Ralph's house now. He tugged gently, and she moved slowly toward him. Behind her, she heard Beth's satisfied laugh.

Will pulled her into the living room, and Beth stepped around them, closing the door behind her. "I'll just go find our host, and let him know we're here." Beth headed in the direction of the dining room, sniffing delightedly. "Smells wonderful!" she exclaimed, though no one seemed to be listening.

Marty stood staring up at Will, transfixed. Her throat was too tight, her mouth too dry, but she had to try to speak. "How . . . ?" Her voice squeaked, then died. She swallowed hard, and tried again. She could feel that same electricity running through her, starting at her fingers, held gently in Will's strong hands. "How did you get here?"

"I got in my truck and drove. It's just across town, you know." The bantering tone, and the light in his eyes gave Marty the answer to the question she had wanted answered, but couldn't bring herself to ask. He was there because he wanted to be with her.

She could feel the walls crumbling. She had worked so hard to build them up again after the last time she had seen him. She needed them to hide behind. But Will was holding her hands, and the electricity he created was blasting through her defenses like they were tissue paper. Her knees felt weak, and she sagged slightly. She would have stumbled, but Will caught her around the waist, and drew her close to him. Then his lips were on hers, and it was as if they were back in his car that first night. His smell, that *right* smell, flooded her nose. Marty reeled with the intensity of the sensation. Heat spread through her, and she returned his kiss with an intensity she hadn't thought possible.

Will loosened his grip on her, and as their lips parted, he pulled back slightly, and looked down at her. "This is real, isn't it, Marty? You feel the same way I do, and it's real, and I'm not letting you go again." He kissed her again, a rain of feather-light caresses across her forehead, her eyes and cheeks and nose, and then back to her mouth, with a hunger that burned in both of them.

Marty pulled away, shaken. "But how did you know? After the last time, I thought I'd never see you again."

"Thank your friend Ralph. I'd been out of town for a few days. He and George set up a dinner meeting while I was gone. I didn't know it was him until I got there.

"I didn't want to listen to him, knowing he was the man I had seen you with, but he can be very adamant when he wants something. He made me see how foolish I had been not to listen to you. I promise you, I will never be that foolish again."

Behind them, someone cleared his throat. Will looked up, and grinned, as Marty turned around to find Ralph and Beth looking at them, and grinning hugely. "Dinner is served, if you'd care to join us?"

Ralph offered his arm to Beth, and they led the way back to the dining room. Marty and Will followed them, their arms twined around each other's waists.

They sat with their chairs close together, as though they couldn't bear to be any distance apart. Through the meal they held hands, unlacing their fingers only long enough to pass serving dishes, or butter their dinner rolls. Neither seemed very interested in the food, and Beth and Ralph carried most of the conversation.

Finally, Ralph filled all their wine glasses, and tapped the side of his glass with his spoon. "May I propose a toast?" He lifted his glass, and they all joined him. "To Marty, one of the best friends a man could have. And to Will, one of the luckiest men I know. Health and happiness to you both."

They drank, and then Ralph continued. "And to Beth. I told Marty her best friend would be beautiful, and I was right. Here's to getting to know each other better."

Beth blushed. Marty could hardly believe it, but *Beth* blushed. She looked back at Ralph, and saw a new light in his eyes. Maybe it was her imagination, but it sure looked like they were getting to know each other pretty well already.

Will raised his glass, and they turned their attention to him. "To Marty's dream house." He saw the stricken look cross her face, and continued hastily. "Not this one, but the one two blocks over, the one that I found last night." His voice thickened to a husky whisper. "The one I want to buy and fix just for you, if you'll let me, if you'll have it. If you'll have me . . ."

Marty's glass slipped from her fingers, and landed, unnoticed on the table, the remaining wine soaking into the tablecloth. Then she was in Will's arms, crying and laughing at the same time. "Yes, Will, yes," she whispered against his neck. "For always."

Beth's laugh, thick with emotion, reached them. Marty turned to look at her friend.

"I think I'll pass on that Caribbean trip, Marty," Beth said. "I have a hunch it'll make a great honeymoon."

About the Author

Christina York has always loved words, in every form. Her first foray into publishing, as the ten-year-old reporter, editor and publisher of a one-page neighborhood newspaper, lasted only a few weeks. During the enforced retirement that followed, she finished grade school, high school, and college, married, had a couple kids, divorced, re-married, and eventually found her way back to writing.

An Oregon native, Christina has always lived on the West Coast. After growing up in the suburbs of L.A., she spent many years in and around Seattle, moved to Eugene, Oregon, and eventually settled on the rugged Oregon coast, where she can see the ocean from her office window. She shares her home with her husband, writer J. Steven York, and a couple of very spoiled cats.